❧ B E A S T ❧

DONNA JO NAPOLI

BEAST

SIMON PULSE

NEW YORK LONDON TORONTO SYDNEY SINGAPORE

ACKNOWLEDGMENTS

For help on earlier drafts, from matters of Islam and Persian history to matters of India and wildlife to matters of storytelling, I thank Barry Furrow, Eva Furrow, Robert Furrow, Nick Furrow, Ayeh Asiaii, Wendy Cholbi, Amani Elkassabany, Elaine Huang, Ruqayya Khan, Emily Manetta, Helen Napoli, Ramneek Pooni, Melissa Running, Roya Salehi, and Richard Tchen. For being such a demanding and kind editorial team, I thank Brenda Bowen, Cylin Busby, and Caitlyn Dlouhy.

First Simon Pulse edition June 2002
Copyright © 2000 by Donna Jo Napoli
Map by Elena Furrow

SIMON PULSE
An imprint of Simon & Schuster
Children's Publishing Division
1230 Avenue of the Americas
New York, NY 10020

Also available in an Atheneum Books for Young Readers hardcover edition.
Designed by Michael Nelson
The text of this book was set in Cochin.

Printed in the United States of America
2 4 6 8 10 9 7 5 3 1

The Library of Congress has cataloged the hardcover edition as follows:
Napoli, Donna Jo, 1948-
Beast / by Donna Jo Napoli.
p. cm.
Summary: Elaborates on the tale of "Beauty and the Beast," told from the point of view of the beast and set in Persia.
ISBN 0-689-83589-2 (hc.)
[1. Fairy tales. 2. Iran—Fiction.] I. Beauty and the beast. English. II. Title.
PZ8.N127 Li 2000
[Fic]—dc21 99-89923
ISBN 0-689-83590-6 (Simon Pulse pbk.)

For Cylin Busby, as she makes the journey for love

CONTENTS

CASPIAN SEA

N
W E
S

MOUNTAINS

TABRIZ

ALBORZ MOUNTAINS

PERSIA

INDUS RIVER

LAKE URUMIYEH

PERSIAN GULF

INDIA

0   100   200   300   400   500
MILES

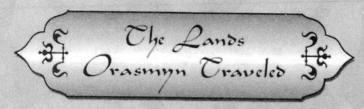

The Lands Orasmyn Traveled

❧ B E A S T ❧

PART I

The Curse

CHAPTER ONE

The Camel

The lion-ape lunges from the tree
a moment too late;
Bahram Chubina's arrow has already
sealed his fate.

I gasp roughly. Beast and warrior glow white, burning, against the gold ground. The sun glints off the
illuminated pages as it glints off the metal *mar*—
snake—that twists around and around from my wrist
to my elbow. My fists clench; I am aghast at dying,
aghast at killing.

"Orasmyn?"

I turn, startled.

Mother comes in, her face unveiled—she has not
yet left the palace this morning. The pleasure of seeing the dark sliver moons under her eyes, her full
cheeks, pulls me at once from the violence on the
page to the sweet calm of our lives.

Beast

Father, the Shah of all Persia, has promised to find me a suitable wife soon. I will be the first adult male outside the young woman's family to ever set eyes on her bare face, to ever know her mysteries. Warmth threads up my throat to my cheeks. I stroke my short beard and smile broad to hide my thoughts.

Mother smiles in return. "You're reading the *Shah-nameh* yet again?" She comes to my reading platform and bends over me. Her hair hangs wavy, freed from the braids that hold it tight at night and that she will rebraid before going outside today. It brushes my arm. With a fingertip she traces the spine of the lion-ape. "His eyes speak anguish."

Her words touch me with their femininity. Women speak through their eyes from behind the *chador*—the veil—that shrouds all else. They are accustomed to listening to the eyes of others, even those whose full faces show.

"Shall I read to you?"

"Battle stories." Mother wrinkles her nose. "I prefer Islamic verse."

"Islamic verse is in Arabic. These are stories in our own strong Persian. And they're not all battle. Let me read to you of Malika falling in love with Shahpour." Already I am thumbing back through the earlier pages.

Mother squats and catches my hand between hers.

"Orasmyn, I've got a present for you. In my room. A book by Saadi."

The prospect intrigues me, for this great mystic, this Sufi, is known for mixing the spirit of Islam with the culture of Persia. But Mother's tone irritates. I pull my hand away. "I don't need help in choosing my reading."

"We all need help, Orasmyn."

"A prince doesn't."

Mother presses her lips together in a thin line. Then her face softens again. "I see you've done your prayers." Her finger now runs the part in the middle of my hair that I made during my cleaning ritual, the *wudhu,* before the prayers that precede sunrise. "Why didn't you come eat with us?" she asks. "Your father and I will be busy with festival duties most of the day. We had hoped to see you this morning, at least."

Today is the Feast of Sacrifices. Every royal family in every town across Persia has invited the poor to partake of the meat from the animal they will sacrifice this noon. Here in Tabriz there will be a double offering, for my family will add a sacrifice of our own to that of the local royal family. "I don't plan to eat on this festival," I say.

"Is that so?" Mother looks at me with curiosity. "You're dressed as a *hajji*—a pilgrim." Fondly, she brushes the folds of cloth on my back.

I draped this white cloth around me as the sun rose. It is almost a year since I returned from my pilgrimage to Mecca. These days, when I go out, I wear my ordinary tunic under royal robes, though of course I carry prayer beads and wear a white hat always. But today I will stand in white cloth with the other *hajjiha,* a cloud of purity. "I'm assisting at the sacrifice."

"Ah." Mother nods. "Then I understand your fasting. But, son, my gentle prince, not every *hajji* must take part."

I hear the question under her words. As a child I ran from the sacrifices, from the spilling of blood. As an adult, I take no part in the hunts. Mother says I am like the flowers that grow in my treasured gardens, more tender than flesh should be.

Still, today I fight off trepidation. The sacrifice is compassionate; as my father's heir, I must understand that. The animal dies to commemorate the ancient sacrifice by Ibrahim. "Don't worry about me." I kiss Mother's hand.

"I'll leave you to prepare, then," she says, straightening up. "At the prayers before the sacrifice, be sure to make your *rakatha*—your bows—deep and low, and to linger a moment before rising. That way I can pick you out from the other *hajjiha* and send you my strength." Mother leaves.

Her strength? A prince should rely on no one.

But it is too late to protest; she is gone.

I open the rear doors, which give directly out to my private garden for praying, my *belaq*. We have palaces in many cities, and I have taken part in designing the gardens at three of them. I work with a cohort of servants, planting, pruning, mulching.

My special fragrance garden around the throne room in the central pavilion of our Isfahan palace is continuously in flower. The carpet I stand on now depicts that garden. The border bands hold daisies and pomegranates and heads of lions. This rug makes my feet want to climb. We winter in Isfahan, of course, on the arid plateau almost completely ringed by mountains.

My yellow roses are at our palace in Shiraz. On the first day of spring, we celebrate Naurouz, New Year's, there, surrounded by flowering persimmons. I always beg Father to take us to Shiraz early, even as early as the end of February, so that we can feel the *bade gulhaye sourkh* — the wind of roses — that blows strong in the afternoon. Processions fill the streets with music and torches for thirty days. I throw coins with lions stamped on them to the people I pass. They throw rose petals in return. All flowers grow in Shiraz, but *gulhaye sourkh* — roses — are what they throw, because the rose is my favorite, Prince Orasmyn's favorite.

But Shiraz is too hot in summer. So we return

north to Tabriz, the capital, where I tend my most extensive gardens.

I step outside now and pass through my walled *belaq* out to the public gardens. To the west stands the mosque. To the south and east and north stretches garden. My eyes follow straight pebbled paths interrupted at regular intervals by a series of steps, on and on, until the paths are lost in the trees and the mountains beyond. It is easy to fool myself into thinking the garden continues forever—infinite.

I imagine I feel a wet breeze from the Caspian Sea to the east—though it is more than a day's journey away. I emerge from the shadows of the portico and walk along a *maddi*—a water channel—to the reflecting pool. The people will gather here after the sacrifice to await the cooked meat. The pavilion on the north side will host the men, while that on the south will host the women. Columns hold up the roofs of the pavilions, columns spaced widely, so that one group can easily see what the other does. The voices will be loud and happy.

But right now the pool and garden are mine. The air is faint with white jasmine. Clover and aromatic grasses crush soft under my bare feet. Sour cherry trees fan out in star designs. I step up onto the *talar*, the platform overlooking the pool, and gaze at the black-and-white limestone colonnades of the palace.

The early sun gives an orangish sheen to the stones, almost the color of henna, and an idea comes to me.

Mother said not every *hajji* must take part in the sacrifice. So nothing should prescribe the participation of those *hajjiha* who do take part. Joyous moment, I am free to choose what duties I assume.

I race to the animal enclosures beyond the mosque, to the camel-holding pen, hoping no one has beat me to the task. Preparing an animal for sacrifice is just as important a part of the feast as slashing its neck.

Kiyumars is already in the pen, stroking the large she-camel. But no one else is about. I join this servant with a silent nod. We've known each other all our lives—we played among the herds of goat and sheep together as children; we tend the gardens of Tabriz side by side as adults—we fall into an easy camaraderie now. Kiyumars puts henna on the head of the camel, turning her the orange color that guided my feet here now. All is well. I rub the camel's eyelids with kohl. She is docile, more docile than I've known a camel to be. Kiyumars takes a sugar lump from his pouch and puts it in the camel's mouth. Ah, now I understand her cooperation, for I have a sweet tooth myself.

The necklace shines from the open box nearby. It is made of tiny mirrors set in red silk with gold embroidered leaves. Carefully I lift it with both hands and hold it under the camel's thick neck. Kiyumars takes one end, and together we fasten the necklace in place. It hangs before her chest like a banner.

Kiyumars dips his hands in the henna again. He turns to the camel, about to rub color into her back, when he gasps.

I look over his shoulder. At first I cannot see it. But now halfway up her single hump a thin line shows, where the hair doesn't lie perfectly flat. It runs two hands-width long.

Kiyumars looks at me with frightened eyes.

We both know what the scar means. Someone cut fat from this camel's hump, a practice of our people for millennia. But now we know, through the teachings of Muhammad, that the Merciful One expressly forbids it: Live animals are never to suffer at the hand of man. An old scar, to be sure. Nevertheless, this camel has been defiled.

"She appeared to be the finest camel, my prince. In the name of the Merciful One, this is truth."

"Was no other camel brought here yesterday and prepared for sacrifice?" I ask, though I can see the holding pen is otherwise empty.

"She is the only one, my prince." Kiyumars' voice shakes. An error regarding sacrifices could call for grave punishment. The local royal family holds to old Persian customs that go against Islam; they would have Kiyumars nailed by his ears to the wall out front of the palace, just as they do to those who break the fast during the monthlong celebration of Ramadhan. I wince at the thought. My hand instinctively takes his upper arm and pulls him close. My chest swells with the need to protect Kiyumars.

But is it written anywhere that a camel who has been violated in this way cannot be sacrificed? I recall no such prohibition, though I have to admit I remember more of the Persian folktales in the *Shahnameh* than of the Arab holy words in the *Qur'an*.

I could ask the *imam*—the prayer leader—just to be sure. But the Feast of Sacrifices is one of the two most important holy days of the lunar year—so the Shah should know the rules that govern it. Likewise, the Shah's son should know. Consultation would be a sign of weakness.

The answer must lie within me.

Think, Orasmyn.

This camel is imperfect. But all the camels in our herd have some defect or other. They have to. Such is the way of the world. This may be the best camel available, despite her scar.

Kiyumars puts both hands to his cheeks, forgetting the henna in his desperation and turning himself orange. "It is my thoughtlessness. Jumail is the only camel prepared for sacrifice. Forgive me, my prince."

Jumail? This is the Arab word for "little camel,"

not the Persian one. This camel clearly belongs to Islam. I reach high and put my hands over her muzzle, trying to pull myself up so I can look into her eyes. The camel stares at me a moment, then blinks and jerks her head away. But she doesn't bare her teeth. Jumail is ready for sacrifice.

I scan my memory for wisdom from the *Qur'an*. "The Merciful One forgives our dietary lapses more easily than most other lapses."

"Yes," says Kiyumars with hope in his voice.

Now I search my memory for wisdom from our people's traditions, wisdom my nursemaid Ava taught me. "And eating camel meat rekindles faith," I say softly.

"The people will be grateful," says Kiyumars. "Especially the sick, my prince."

I think of the sick, for whom half the meat of this camel will be salted and set aside. They will chew it all year long for strength no other meat can give. Nothing would be gained by failing to sacrifice this beast.

And I cannot believe the Merciful One would want Kiyumars to suffer for an innocent oversight. Indeed, if animals are not to suffer at the hand of man, how then can humans be allowed such suffering?

I fasten a necklace of bells around the camel, high

up and tight, so that it rides in front of the arch of her neck. Then I stand tall before my servant, my friend.

Kiyumars bows to me. When he rises, he smears the camel's hump with henna, putting extra on the scar that disappeared with his first swipe. I add a strand of precious stones between the necklace of bells and the necklace of mirrors. After Kiyumars finishes coloring the camel's back, I spread the fine Kashmir shawl across her. She is ready.

Everything has been done correctly.

Or almost everything.

In an instant I am cold. It is nearly impossible to be cold anywhere in my country in the summer, even at the start of summer, even in Tabriz. Yet I shiver now. It is as though a tiny being flutters around my head, blowing and blowing. It as as though a storm begins.

CHAPTER TWO

The Pari

The bazaar is thronged with the faithful, as always. But this morning they do not barter for cloth or copper vessels, for wool or carpets. And this morning the number of people is multiplied many times, for the women have come out of their homes to stand beside the men, and the *zarehun*—the farmers—have left the fields to take their place along the sides of the road. All have come out for the procession.

Little boys run before the *hajjiha*—the pilgrims—picking up small stones and sticks. Normally they use brooms to sweep the streets, but on the Feast of Sacrifices no brooms are allowed, because the broken needles left behind by sweeping might pierce the bare feet of the *hajjiha*. I am grateful; many times on my pilgrimage I walked for days. But I've been home long enough that my feet have grown tender again.

Behind the row of *hajjiha* comes the ram to be sacrificed by the local royals. Next comes the camel to be sacrificed by the Shah. A gap follows these two animals, a gap in which the bells of their necklaces jingle, happy and light. If they know they are to die, they must be filled with rapture at the prospect. To give one's life for the Merciful One, that is true privilege.

After the gap come the music makers: the men blowing *saz*—oboes—my favorite instruments, besides the human voice, that is. And one man playing the *kerna*—a trumpet as tall as he is. And then a row of men on kettledrums. This music isn't new. We hear it every night and at all festivals. And during the month of Ramadhan, we hear it before each dawn. Familiarity endears it to me. This is the music of my faith. I listen to it from my position far in the front of the procession and it is muted, like the sound of water in a river on the far side of a stand of trees. A smile swells my cheeks, though this is a solemn feast.

I know the Shah comes immediately behind the music makers, flanked by his most loyal servants. When we travel long distances, my father rides in the caravan with Mother. I used to ride there with them when I was young. But in processions, Father sits on a horse. Today it is a white horse, an Arabian, accustomed to the sands.

I was with Father when the messenger brought

this horse as an advance gift from one of the guests who will arrive tonight or early tomorrow for the weeklong hunt Father has organized. An even longer hunt will be arranged for the end of summer. A white horse augurs well; Father plans to ride it in the hunt. Today its tail is dyed red, along with the tails of all the other royal horses. I imagine the horse now, red tail held high, head higher. Father in his high crown, his *taj*, astride that horse—what a magnificent sight; Mother's heart must be near bursting from pride as she sits on the carpet in the caravan.

I hear the cries of the people who break jars and scatter the sugar that was in them beneath the feet of the royal horses. They wish my family well.

Then come the local royals, greeted warmly by the crowds, but not quite as warmly as the Shah, of course.

We stop at the appointed place in the street. Two barrels of water await us, two shining daggers, many empty bowls. The *hajjiha* surround the sheep and camel. The music makers back into the crowd. The royalty stops and dismounts.

Now it is the turn of the mourners. The rest of us stay silent as the castanets click. Men with their heads plastered in mud kneel and throw dirt upon themselves. Women loosen their braids and scratch their own faces. The penitents join them; flagellants nick the front of their heads; blood streams down their chests. They beseech the Merciful One to purify them.

I am cold again—that sudden, inexplicable cold that seized me in the holding pen with Kiyumars this morning. I look around at the crowd. A peasant rubs the amulet that hangs from his neck to protect against the evil eye. The woman standing next to him touches the wrist of her small daughter, then puts her hand on the ground to transfer any evil that would prey on her child into the harmless, unharmable dirt. We are all quivering at the sight of so much sorrow—the penitents' sorrow.

At last the calamity criers grow quiet. I fold my hands in front of me and step to the side as the other *hajjiha* turn the sheep and the camel toward Mecca. A barrel of water is set before each animal. They drink greedily. The sheep stops quickly, but the camel keeps drinking, in her huge capacity. She drinks half the barrel and is still going. People fidget; the camel drinks. If she finishes the barrel, that might mean she could have drunk even more. It is wrong to sacrifice an animal without first giving it cool waters to slake its thirst. Compassion allows for no less.

I step forward and look into the barrel. The camel has drunk three-fourths of the water and is still drinking. Drinking and drinking. The *hajjiha* instinctively move closer together. The camel lifts her head from the barrel, and the sun glints off the drops caught in her muzzle hairs. The *hajji* on the other side of the camel peeks into the barrel now. He turns to us and nods; the camel has been satisfied, and water still remains. As the *hajji* beside me lets out a sigh, I realize I, too, have been holding my breath.

Now two *hajjiha* pick up the daggers and take their posts beside the animals. The *imam* steps to the front and leads us in prayer. We make our bows to thank the Merciful One for accepting the sacrifice. I bow, too, but I rise quickly, careful not to linger. If Mother is watching, she will not be able to pick me out from the other *hajjiha;* she cannot try to send me her strength. My own strength thickens my arms and neck.

The camel throws her head up, takes a step backward. Perhaps she sensed the change in the crowd? Perhaps she's seen what a dagger can do? In this instant, I know her fear. My hand reaches out to rest on her flank, a feeble attempt to console her.

The daggers make a single gash to the neck. I fight the urge to look away. My throat, my cheeks, my eyes sting with sympathy. I force myself to keep my hand on her flank.

The sacrifice is good; neither the head of the sheep nor that of the camel is severed. The blood is caught in the huge pottery bowls held beneath the wounds. The sweet smell of the blood turns my stomach. All the *hajjiha*, all of us together, help the animals sink to their knees, then, finally, rest on their sides.

A spasm shakes the belly of the huge camel. My hands want to comfort her again; I kneel on them to hold them back, for comfort now would be inappropriate—this death is sacred.

The Kashmir shawl on the camel's back comes away. My throat tightens in worry, but the scar on her hump is invisible. Her eyes stay open—even the inner eyelid that protects against blowing desert sands doesn't lower. Yet she is dead, for the *hajji* who held his hand on her heart has withdrawn.

The butchers have already begun their work. The skins are peeled off carefully. They will be saved for a rug, in the case of the sheep, and vests and shoes, in the case of the camel. Now the butchers pull out the intestines and coil them into bowls. They will be dried, and pieces will be given to anyone who wants to attach them to a wall to ward off the evil eye, a custom that goes back centuries, long before Islamic times. The right eye of the sheep is scooped out. It, also, will be dried, then sewn into the bonnet of the new baby in the local royal family, to ban ill luck. Women come forward now with armfuls of cotton. They soak up the sheep and camel blood.

The royal cooks skewer the *halal* meat—the sacrificial meat—on sticks and carry it to the pits specially prepared in my garden. The people follow in two streams along the street, the men on one side, the women on the other.

I walk without speaking to anyone, absorbed in the crowd. Gradually I slough off the sadness in my heart that comes at every sacrifice.

We pass the tavern run by Christians, who look out the window at us. I look back with equal interest. The writings of Rumi, the best-loved mystic of Islam, teaches that all religions are true: Muslim, Christian, Hindu, Buddhist, Jew — all worship the one and only God. Still, I don't know any of the faces in that tavern — I've never had a Christian friend. Often the tavern clients raise a glass in greeting to the passers on the street, but no one dares salute today. The Feast of Sacrifices sobers everyone.

Four years ago, when I was thirteen, Father's right-hand man, Shahpour, took me to the taverns a month after my circumcision. I tasted Christian wine, and Hebrew wine, too, though intoxicating drink is forbidden to all Islam. The Merciful One tries not to burden his faithful unduly with restrictions that are hard to obey, and He is all merciful in accepting us back when we have strayed. That straying was an experience to remember, or so said Shahpour. I fell asleep and had to be carried home; I can remember only the beginnings of the evening.

The Curse

I am walking around the perimeter of the palace now. Enormous vats hang over open fires. The better parts of the mutton and camel meat are being roasted or salted for drying; the stomach and tails are boiling for the servants; and all the rest has gone into stews in these vats. *Ghorme sabzi:* minced parsley and cilantro, fenugreek and mint, all fried in olive oil, then cubes of meat simmered, then water and red beans added on top. All will be served on a bed of rice. The smell makes my mouth water. Fasting isn't required today, even of the *hajjiha* who actually slay the animals. Fasting is required only during the daylight hours of Ramadhan—fasting and contemplation. But most of the *hajjiha* who assisted at the sacrifice today will fast, I'm sure.

I breathe in the aromas of the meal, lingering especially over the many deserts made with honey. I love the candies of honey and almond the best.

Fasting is difficult. But that's what makes it worth doing. Discipline, self-restraint, generosity toward those who truly lack the necessities of life—that's what fasting is about.

The prayer leader's assistant cries out the *adhan*— the call to prayer—from the minaret, the tall mosque tower. Everyone takes a turn at the basins of fresh water that are lined up along the edges of the pavilion just for that purpose; we wash our face and hands and run our wet fingers through the middle of our hair and over the tops of our feet. We face Mecca and make four *rakatha,* offering the midday prayers, our lips almost touching the ground, speaking softly to the world.

Men sit in circles around the *sophreh* — the sheets on the floor — careful to keep our feet from touching the cloth. Servants come with pots of rice, followed by others with pots of stew. They prepare the bowls at each table, rice on the bottom, stew piled high on top. When a bowl is offered to me, I find the strength to resist; I pass it on to the next man.

The women harpists take their positions at one corner of the pavilion. Though they are almost completely covered, their femininity prevails in the graceful music. They play harmoniously. Baskets of candies sit on the floor beside them, for the taking. I think of the sugar Kiyumars fed the camel as we dressed her for the sacrifice.

Sugar on a tongue, on my tongue, on a woman's tongue.

I excuse myself and walk the path, through the arch over the entrance to the walled park, out toward the Alborz Mountains. Mount Damavand looms in the distance, the air above it calm, though I know the earth within it can burn and bubble out and over its peak, down its sides. Once, a visiting Frenchman, gazing upon our volcano, told Father it reminded him of Frenchwomen. He said they give the perfume of roses—and French roses are the best in the world—but they consume like lava.

Though he spoke in his own tongue, not my Persian tongue, I understood what he said, because I've studied Latin and the French of Paris, along with Arabic and Greek and Turkish, since I was small. The latter three languages, naturally, are essential for religious and commerce purposes. But Father believes it is impossible to know the heads of Europeans if you can't speak Latin, and impossible to know their hearts if you can't speak French.

I listened intently. I didn't believe what he said about French roses, of course, for how could they be better than my beloved *gulhaye sourkh*? But the part about women, that fascinated me.

The women of my country are not volcanic, I don't think. Oh, they are full of secrets to be discovered. But their secrets are like the secrets of the earth. The vale of Kashmir, in the eastern part of Persia, looks bleak and dead in the autumn. The fields turn silver. But I have walked through those fields; I have knelt among the diminutive lavender blossoms; my hands have swept away the brush from around the autumn wild crocuses with their orange-red stigmata and styles—the source of saffron. Sweet; savory; *sabzi*—spices. I will enjoy discovering my wife's secrets, learning her perfumes.

"Prince! Prince Orasmyn!" Kiyumars runs up the path. "You can't go walking so far."

I stopped at his first words, but now I walk again. It is not right that Kiyumars should tell me what I can or cannot do. I stretch my neck long in irritation.

"It isn't safe, my prince," calls Kiyumars. He arrives at my side. "Come back with me."

His earnestness brushes away my irritation. I laugh. "Isn't safe?"

Kiyumars pants as he catches his breath. "They've brought in lions and tigers from India."

"What do you mean?"

"For the hunt, my prince. The Shah has vowed to kill a lion with his bare hands."

I know that boast. Long ago lions roamed the plateaus of Persia, not just far in the east, near India, like today. Ancient kings—Darius and his son Xerxes and so many others—took pride in wounding them with arrows, then strangling them with their hands. I don't need to imagine the vile scene, for the *Shahnameh* has illustrations. Why, Bahram Gur even hunted down the dreadful karg, the legendary beast with a single horn long as a sword. Courage in the hunt is much valued.

As of tomorrow, I will need to make scarce of myself, so as not to shame my father in front of his friends. My dear father, who loves me so, turns away in disgust when I refuse invitations to join the hunt. He says if I can thrill to hunt and battle on the pages of books, then I should thrill to it on the field.

I am already walking quickly back toward the palace, Kiyumars dashing along with me. In this hunting park there is no end to peacocks and ostriches, deer and wild boar. But Father likes to make his blood rush now and then. That's what he said to me the last time he brought in beasts of prey for the hunt. This park is so large that wild animals can be set loose, and still the game is difficult. Indeed, the last time beasts were brought here, the hunters saw neither the lion nor the tiger. The Indian servants had to catch them again and take them away after the week's hunt ended. For them it was easy: Indian hunting servants learn the ways of wild cats in childhood; their land overruns with lions and tigers.

Kiyumars looks over his shoulder, the whites of his eyes large.

"The beasts are deep in the hunting park, Kiyumars," I say. "No one will see them today."

Kiyumars blinks at me. "You're right, my prince. Tomorrow, though, the hunters will face the beasts."

"I doubt it."

"Our Indian guests are coming with elephants specially trained to drive prey toward hunters. The servants have spent days filling barrels with water for them."

Ah, so Father won't allow a repeat disappointment; this time he'll kill his lion.

We pass under the arch and out of the park. I turn to the north.

"Dare I ask where you're going, my prince?"

"I believe you've just asked, Kiyumars." I laugh again at the worry on his face. Perhaps when I am Shah, Kiyumars will be my right-hand man just as Shahpour is to Father now. "Don't worry. I'll stay in the fruit and flower gardens."

Kiyumars bows and leaves as I walk along paths beside a *maddi* filled with mountain water that runs so fast, it sings. The low mud walls around the garden I enter now could never hold back a lion. I pass *derakhte badam*—almond trees—and *anar*—pomegranates. I pass lotus trees, the symbol of fertility. If I were not fasting, I would chew on a *beh daneh*—quince seed—and the bitter aphrodisiac *sendjed*—Bohemian olive. This fruit-tree garden is sacred to me, thus I call it by the Arabic word—it is my *jannat,* my own Garden of Paradise. The *maddi* runs into a small, round pool with carved stones at the edges. I enjoy the scene: black rams chasing one another. The carver was playful.

My stomach growls. During the fasting of Ramadhan I always get through the daylight hours without eating by taking a nap in the afternoon. Now I lie on the ground beside the pool and close my eyes.

The *adhan* wakes me, calling and calling from the minaret. It's late afternoon already, time for prayer. I wash my face in the pool. I wash the tops of my feet. I run my hands through my hair. I look in the waters.

The face of the camel shimmers.

I squeeze my eyes shut, shake my head, then look again.

The camel lifts her upper lip. "Each animal has its way," comes the watery voice.

My heart leaps to my throat. I want to look around, to search the bushes for the source of this voice, but my eyes hold fast now, they cannot stray. Everything in me knows: It is the reflection of the camel itself that speaks. The truth of the moment envelops me. My shock gives way to reverence. "Each animal has its way," I echo.

"The stork is pious. The crab is tenacious. The panther is proud and jealous."

I know this. I know the way of each animal. Mother has told me these things, as every mother in my country tells her children. I am sick at what I know must come next. My mouth is dry, my throat parched. I lower my lips to the water, meeting the camel's muzzle. If only I could drink.

"The camel . . . say it, Prince Orasmyn . . . the camel . . ."

"The camel is vindictive," I whisper, my own words trapping me. There has to be a way out. Perhaps I was wrong; perhaps the water holds not a spirit itself, but the image of a spirit standing behind me. I throw water over my shoulder and chant, "The dead are thirsty, be comforted, the dead are thirsty, be comforted."

"I already drank my fill," comes that voice.

I fall back on my heels and rock myself. This spirit will accept no comfort.

But, oh, the Merciful One is watching. He must be. I spring to my feet and begin my *rakatha* four. I press not only my forehead to the ground, but my nose and chin; I grovel in the dirt. In my fear I recall the teachings of my nursemaid Ava: I spit over my left shoulder, then my right, so the lurking devil won't distract me.

When I finish, I can't stop myself from kneeling and looking in the water again. My people speak of *parian*—fairies—who can be malicious or benevolent. The Zoroastrians believed malicious *parian* punished bad people and benevolent *parian* aided good people. Though I hold no Zoroastrian beliefs, even the *Qur'an* tells of *djinn*, spirits that cannot be seen in their own form, but can take on disguises. The *Qur'an* records the exact words of the Merciful One as spoken through the Angel Gabriel to the last true prophet

Muhammad; these spirits surround us. Many of them protect the creatures of the earth. "Did you protect the camel?" I ask the image in the pool.

"As poorly as you did," comes the answer.

"I am sorry," I whisper.

"You sacrificed a beast who knew suffering."

I see the thin line of the scar across the camel's hump. "Yes," I breathe. "I'm sorry."

"All involved must pay retribution."

"No," I say quickly. Not Kiyumars. Please not Kiyumars. "I am the one who made the decision to sacrifice the camel in spite of the scar. It is my responsibility. Solely mine."

"This is true. You consulted no one." The camel's lip raises in a sneer again. "Prince that you are."

I nod. "No one must pay but me."

"You were tested, Orasmyn. A royal test. And you failed."

Awe and dread twist my insides. "I will study the *Qur'an* better. I will memorize all the rules. I will—"

"You understand nothing. Recount the five basic principles of faith in your head."

"I am recounting them," I say.

"Tomorrow your father will slay you, as you have slain the camel. Today you suffer that knowledge. You suffer, like the camel."

My hands grasp at the water, come away empty,

grasp again. The image disappears. "Come back. Don't curse me so." I jump into the pool, reaching with both arms under the water. "Come back." I thrash every which way.

Finally, I stand quiet.

I recount the five basic principles of faith, the fourth of which fills my head to the bursting point: Your actions will be rewarded or punished by divine justice.

The water is still.

CHAPTER THREE

Kooma

The townsfolk have left, probably hours ago. But the hunting guests are arriving in droves. I run to the men's pavilion.

Shahpour, Father's most trusted companion, leans against a column, talking. In his hands is a white cup. "A treasure," he says, holding it before his eyes. He bows in gratitude. "The Shah has none carved so beautifully."

The Indian guest in front of him bows, as well. "Even the most powerful poison is rendered harmless if drunk from rhinoceros horn. A man as powerful as the Shah can use such protection."

What else can rhinoceros horn protect against? And what other preventive measures does this guest know? But my goal now is to find Father as quickly as possible. I pass them and walk through the pavilion, searching.

"Orasmyn, is that you?" Ardeshir, a member of the royal family of Ashraf, takes me by the upper arms. "All wet? Don't tell me you've been fighting a water dragon in Lake Urumiyeh." He laughs and reaches out to a man near him. "This is the Shah's son. Look, Bahram. Lake Urumiyeh may be too salty for fish, but our Orasmyn has hunted down a dragon there. He rivals your namesake in bravery."

I greet the man called Bahram, named after the greatest hunter among the *Shahnameh* heroes: Bahram Gur killed a dragon that devoured a youth. That's what Ardeshir is joking about now. "Have you seen the Shah?" I ask, barely controlling my urgency.

"He's risen high," says Ardeshir mysteriously. When I look at him in bewilderment, he laughs again. "The Indian guests brought three elephants, each more enormous than the last. The Shah rides upon the neck of the hugest one."

I look past the people in the pavilion, past the pigeon tower, toward the fields, where an elephant lumbers with my father. I run toward him.

But, no. What if I startle the animal and it tramples me? I see myself lying crumpled all night and my father in the morning killing me out of compassion. The *pari*'s curse can be realized many ways.

I run back to the pavilion. "Ardeshir, will you come with me to see my father now? I desire your presence." I turn to Bahram. "Will you come, too? In the name of the Merciful One, I invite you both."

"Of course, my prince." Ardeshir takes in my face, which must speak volumes, for he blinks as though frightened himself. "Let us go."

The men flank me and we walk toward Father, waving our arms slowly to catch his attention without alarming the elephant.

My caution turns out to be unnecessary. The huge bull elephant goes down on one front knee, then the other, exhibiting its perfect training. His eyes look ancient, though I guess he is no more than forty years old. Father throws his leg across the bull's head to one side and slides off. The bull takes advantage of the moment to dig his tusks into the earth, then he stands again and forages among the overturned roots with that one fingerlike protrusion at the end of his trunk.

Father comes close, his eyes bright with the excitement of guests, of preparation for the hunt he loves. "What is it, my son? Have you fallen into one of our great Persian rivers?" Father raises his brows playfully. Persia has no major rivers, a fact that makes transportation across our land more tedious than in many others. But Father has a happy spirit; he often makes light of our lackings.

I want to tell him about the curse; impatience almost loosens my tongue. But now I realize it was a mistake to enlist Ardeshir and Bahram. Father and I need to talk privately—until then I must calm myself. "I waded in the pool of the fruit-tree garden," I say, plucking at the wet cloth that clings to my chest.

"Something this elephant could appreciate," says Father.

"What a magnificent beast." Bahram reaches out, as though to touch a tusk. The bull turns his head toward him. Bahram retreats rapidly. "They painted him well."

The elephant's head is decorated in reds and blues and yellows, fanning out from a central line down his trunk in symmetric swirls. Even the fronts of his ears are painted. His legs are broad like pillars—he could hold high any faith. The nails on his feet are huge, and several are split in the middle at the lower edge. He is used to walking on hard earth; crossing our desert must have been difficult.

Ardeshir smiles. "When I saw you from afar, sitting straight and tall on his massive neck, I thought of our people's hero Rustam, sitting on his brave and giant horse Raksh."

"Exactly my thought," says Bahram.

Fear rushes to my chest anew. Rustam's adventures in the *Shahnameh* are inscribed in my mind, all of them, including his downfall. The colossal Rustam, with the height of eight men standing on one another's shoulders, made the error of sleeping with a Turan woman. Only once, but once was enough. Many years later, Rustam was in battle against a Turan warrior. He thrust a dagger in the warrior's chest, and in the moment before the young man died, father and son finally recognized each other.

"Look at me." The words burst from my mouth on their own. "Oh, Father, look well at me."

"I am looking, my son."

"Do you recognize me?"

"Of course." Father shakes his head in confusion, clearly not thinking of Rustam's grave flaw, of his tragic destiny.

"Remember who I am tomorrow, Father. Remember tomorrow."

"I will always know who you are." Father puts his arms around me and hugs tight, ignoring my wet clothing. He whispers in my ear, "Whether you ever hunt or not, Orasmyn, you are my beloved son." His voice is gentle.

I know this. And now I think of Kiyumars, who might be cursed as well, who might also be slated for death at Father's hand. "Promise me," I whisper into his ear, "promise that tomorrow you will kill no man — no matter who that man may be."

Father leans back just the slightest bit and tilts his head until our foreheads meet. "I have no intention of killing anything but the game in the hunting park."

"Nevertheless, promise me. No matter what you may think the man has done. No matter what anyone else says to you. No matter what. You cannot kill a man tomorrow, friend or foe, royalty or servant."

"I promise. But tell me, son, what do you fear?"

"I've been told you will kill . . . someone tomorrow. Someone you don't want to kill."

"I will kill no one!" Father's arms flex across my back. "Come talk to me later. Tonight. Explain what this is all about."

Father keeps promises. His words should wrap me in safety. Yet this promise brings no respite. My teeth clench.

The bull elephant trumpets.

The blare is astonishing, resounding. All of us run.

"Do not be afraid," calls a slim boy with a red turban. He speaks in halting Arabic. He has come running from the animal holding pen. "Kooma saw me and gave greeting. That is all." The boy bows to the ground, then gets up and dashes past, to the great elephant. He pulls a long stalk of *naishakar* — sugarcane — from the cloth bag that hangs across his shoulder.

The elephant Kooma chomps the stalk. It disappears into his mouth in jerks.

"That's Abdullah," says the Shah. "He trained Kooma for the hunt."

"Is that so?" says Bahram.

Abdullah bows. "I have the honor of being Kooma's *mahout*," he says, using the word from his native Indian tongue. "I am his caretaker and trainer for life. Come, Kooma, show your respect." He slaps the elephant low on the trunk.

Kooma stretches his trunk forward a tremendous length.

We step farther back.

Abdullah smiles. "He is showing off. An Indian elephant has a much longer trunk than an African one."

"So you are his *mahout*. How does one train an elephant?" asks Ardeshir, approaching the elephant once more.

Abdullah bows to Ardeshir now. "Is it permitted that I work as we talk?"

"Certainly," says the Shah.

We come close, so we can listen easily. Elephants are native to much of India, but not to Persia. None of us is very familiar with them, I venture.

Abdullah takes a half coconut shell out of his cloth bag and scrapes Kooma's skin in larger and larger circles. "A bull is more difficult to train," he says proudly. "I walked Kooma back and forth between two trained cows to teach him obedience."

"And when he did not obey . . . ?" asks Ardeshir.

"Kooma loves sugarcane."

The men laugh.

I cannot laugh. My mind is on the camel, Jumail, who loved sugar lumps, on the image of that camel in the pool waters.

Abdullah scrapes more vigorously with the coconut shell. He goes around to the other side of Kooma. We hear the noise of the shell on the thick, wrinkled skin. Kooma takes a step forward, a step backward, rocking his enormous weight in obvious pleasure. His eyes close.

The power of this beast commands my attention. Kooma opens his eyes and seems to look right at me. His gaze is cold, as though he knows of my wrongdoing to the camel, as though he would do me harm. It takes all my willpower not to back away.

Abdullah passes under Kooma's legs and out to our side again. I realize he did that simply to impress us. He flashes stained black teeth in a grin; his gums are red from chewing betel leaves. Then he takes a flask and cloth from his bag. He walks along Kooma's side dribbling oil. The olive smell is so rich, it cuts through the grassy scent of elephant. Abdullah swabs Kooma's skin with the oil, moving the cloth in those circles again. "I set dogs loose to yap and run around Kooma's legs."

"Did they dare to go under him, like you did?" I ask.

Abdullah looks at me with bright eyes. He's happy

to have his little display of bravery—or reckless-ness—acknowledged. "These dogs do not think of risk. That is why they are good at the hunt. They face tigers without retreating."

"But Kooma doesn't have to take on the dogs, surely," says Bahram.

"Kooma must work with the dogs. He needs to work well, not be disturbed. He must not flinch when they bark."

"And Kooma learned this easily?" asks Ardeshir.

"Kooma is even-mannered, though he is but twenty years old."

"Twenty," I say. "Is that all? He's so tall, I thought he must be twice that."

"He will be the grand old man when he is forty," says Abdullah. "He will retire by then." He goes around Kooma's other side to spread the oil and rub again.

"So the dogs don't flinch around tigers and Kooma does not flinch around the dogs." The Shah walks close and puts a hand on Kooma's trunk, looking up into his eye. "But how will Kooma act around tigers?"

Abdullah comes under Kooma's belly again. He puts the flask and cloth away in his bag. "Kooma leads the hunt in the Gir Forest, where both tigers and lions prey. He has earned the title Kooma the Brave."

"Good. For tomorrow I fulfill my destiny as ruler of

all Persia. Tomorrow these hands kill a lion." The Shah brushes elephant dirt from his palms. He turns to me. "We will talk later. Don't forget. For now, let us go back and greet the guests who are still arriving."

"And enjoy the guests who have already arrived," says Ardeshir.

"To be sure, my good friend." The Shah walks toward the pavilion with Ardeshir at his side and Bahram behind him.

I can hear Ardeshir talking about the habits of lions, and Father exclaiming in interest. I don't want them to go off without me, especially Father, yet I am drawn to the elephant. To the skin that now glistens with oil. To the eyes that seem so small in that weighty head.

"Do not be afraid," says Abdullah, the same words he said when he ran past us before.

This elephant is mild-mannered, well trained. But Abdullah is right: I feel danger. Life-threatening danger. It is not the curse of the *pari* that alarms me now, though that torment lies in wait in the back of my mind until I can speak with Father alone tonight. No, the danger I sense in this moment comes from Kooma.

"Touch him."

I dare to put my hand on Kooma's trunk where Father put his. Kooma waits. Both my hands run down his tusk. The tip is jagged. Fear shoots from the back of my neck, up behind my ears. I walk around the front of Kooma and inspect the other tusk. It ends sharp but smooth.

Abdullah is at my shoulder. "He may have hit a large rock when he was digging for roots once. Or he may have broken the tip of that tusk in a battle with another bull."

"Would he battle a lion or a tiger?"

"His job is to drive them out of their hiding places toward the hunters."

"But if he had to, would he battle a lion or a tiger?"

"He would not back down."

"Would he battle a man?"

Abdullah's face goes slack. His eyes grow guarded. "You have nothing to fear from Kooma. He is well trained."

I nod. "Thank you, Abdullah, for the reassurance." I turn my back on the beast and run as fast as I can after the men. I must stay by Father's side until we have a chance to speak. And in the meantime, I must rack my brain for a way to undo the *pari*'s curse.

CHAPTER FOUR

The Plan

We are seated in the garden pavilion, clusters of men on the floor, talking with our heads almost touching. I don't want to be here—despite my fasting today, all hunger has fled in the wake of the curse. My entire body is tense with the effort of playing host. And a poor host I am, anyway, for the curse has deafened my ears so that these men have to repeat what they say to me several times before I finally understand and give an appropriate, if brief, response.

The smell of *sib*—apple—permeates the breath of the rich Persian merchant to my left. He must have chewed the dry fruit on his journey here, for our midday meal had no apple. I smell *syah-dane*—fennel—on the breath of the Indian man to my right. His teeth are as black from chewing these seeds as the teeth of Abdullah, the elephant trainer. And maybe, just maybe, his breath also carries a hint of *sir*—garlic. I never eat garlic or even onions, unless they are cooked until they become transparent and their sweetness emerges. I heed the old Persian warning against the way hot spices can excite the flesh. Hindus heed this warning, too, or so I thought. Our guest must be daring.

The *adhan* sounds, at last. Sunset comes late at this time of summer. The men have been waiting for the call to prayers, so that they can eat once more.

I am here in this pavilion for my private reason: Kiyumars. I searched for him this afternoon and I couldn't find him. He's likely to help in serving the dinner meal now, though. I have to talk with him—I have to find out if the *pari* sought him out, after all—if he, too, is cursed because of my poor decision. And if so, what the nature of that curse may be. I must help him.

The men around me rise as one and perform the *wudhu* in the water basins, which have been refilled with fresh water. We bow, only three *rakatha* this time. The ritual prayers cover me, like a cloak. The smell of *abghosht*—mutton on the bone cooked with white beans and spinach—brings tears to my eyes. This food would have been delicious to the innocent self I was but yesterday, the self who deserved nourishment.

The rice is served in large bowls. I look around. Kiyumars is at the far end of the pavilion, ladeling *abghosht* from the cooking vat into serving bowls. I get up from my place on the floor and walk around the outside of the pavilion, the muscles of my stomach tightening so hard, I think I may double over. My feet rush at the last moment, so that I knock another servant boy, who falls against Kiyumars' arm. Kiyumars laughs good-naturedly. He looks at me in surprise. "My prince?"

I back off, shaking my head at Kiyumars' obvious lightheartedness. I am alone in this curse, at least. The *pari* has spared Kiyumars. At least that. My relief is sharply lonely.

Shahpour puts his arm around my waist from behind. "Come, Orasmyn. Your father waits for you."

Father, at last. I clasp Shahpour's hand in both mine. "Where?"

"In the mosque." Shahpour looks at me strangely. "Are you all right, my prince?"

I free myself from his arm and hurry along the path.

A servant girl walks by with a basket of fresh dates and figs sitting on slices of cucumber. I snatch a handful of the dates. I stare at them, momentarily off balance from my own sudden impulse. My fast should not end until tomorrow. But these dates lure me. And, yes, for good reason: Dates are a remedy against poisons and certain sorceries. Thanks be to the Merciful One for allowing me to take this path, to pass by this servant girl. I bite a date, then shove all of them into my mouth. I can barely chew, my mouth is so full. The sugary juice shocks my tongue. My stomach constricts with the need for more—for a whole meal.

The mosque has four *iwanha*—deeply vaulted arched portals. I wipe date juice from my beard with my open hand, then enter through the *iwan* closest to the palace. Father's shoes are pushed neatly against the entrance wall. The basins of water that always stand at the ready for the faithful glow gold in a faint light. Father is seated on the carpet in the *mihrab*—the niche in the wall that faces Mecca. This is where the *imam* stands to deliver his sermon during the Friday prayer service. The curved walls of the *mihrab* help reflect his voice so that even the women in the mezzanine above can hear. Now, though, the mosque is empty, but for Father and me.

A candle burns nearby and lights up Father's face and the Arabic calligraphy on the wall behind him. Ants attack the dead body of an *aqrab*—a scorpion— in the corner. I hurry to the carpet and sit on my heels.

"Speak, Orasmyn."

"I am cursed."

"Who cursed you?"

"A *djinn*," I say, using the word of the *Qur'an* here in the mosque rather than the word *pari* of my people.

"I allowed a defiled camel to be sacrificed today. I brought the curse upon myself."

"You had a reason for this?" Father's voice is steady, but I saw his involuntary wince when I said the word *djinn.* And he cannot hide the small twitch of his lips.

"I had a reason. But I was wrong."

Father sits silent for a moment. He never would have had the poor judgment I displayed this morning. He would have known the exact words of the *Qur'an.* He would have followed the ritual in every detail. He would have known what a Shah should know, what a Shah's son should know. I look away in shame, as much as fear.

"The sacrifice is to the Merciful One, not to any *djinn,*" says Father at last.

I turn back quickly to him.

"It is for the Merciful One to forgive, in his infinite compassion," says Father. "It is for the Merciful One to quell the *djinn's* curse." He leans toward me until his eyes are only a hand's distance from mine. "What is this curse?"

"You will kill me tomorrow."

Father's breath escapes with a groan. "I feared this. When you spoke so strangely today, I feared this." He clenches his jaw, and I see a muscle ripple along the right side of his jawline. He takes the candle and holds it close to the carpet. "This was woven in neighboring Heriz."

My eyes follow the moving candle flicker.

"These canals abound with fish. These gardens are decorated with birds and deer and flowering shrubs and blossoms. A peaceful garden. One that you, my son, might have designed." His fingertips run like animal feet across the weft of red and yellow cotton. "See here?" Father's fingers trace the brocading of silver and gold silk on the thin wool pile. "Ducks lie in waiting for the fish to swim around the corner." He looks up at me again. "But the fish never do."

My lungs swell with the determination in his voice. I leap ahead of his words to their intent — for I am the prince, I should find my own solution. "I will lock myself in my room. I will let no man enter after midnight."

"Excellent," says Father. "Stay within and pray. The Merciful One will hear you." Father holds the fist of his right hand cradled in the palm of his left. "I will enlist Shahpour. He'll lock me in my own room with your mother, who will likewise lock me in her arms. And in the morning, Shahpour will come get me and stay by my side all through the hunt."

"How long will we keep apart, Father?"

"The *djinn* said I would kill you tomorrow, precisely tomorrow?"

"Those were the words."

"Then you must pray all day, Orasmyn. And I must not come anywhere near you until after midnight tomorrow."

"Yes," I say, listening to his words, words that match my plan exactly. If only we can hold firm to this plan, we can thwart the *pari*'s curse.

"Be in your room by the last ritual prayer tonight."

"I'm going immediately."

We hug.

I exit quickly, rushing past the bookshelves, out through the same *iwan* I entered by. Two men walk the path toward me. But I can tolerate no delay. I duck into the shadows of the mosque and pad along its side, then cross the *ziyada*—the outer court—and run over the dirt that still holds the sun's warmth. The crowds will be easy to skirt around if I make a route through the rose garden. I run in that direction, my feet growing lighter as my hope grows. Already I am promising myself that I will not stop at the fourth *rakat* in the evening's prayers. Tonight I will keep bowing and praying and bowing and praying until I fall asleep on the floor of my room. My plan is good. We will not fail.

"Pssst."

I stop. "Who's there?"

"Ahi! You're a man. I heard only footsteps. I didn't

know." The woman's voice comes from beyond the rosebushes just ahead.

A woman shouldn't go alone in the garden. She is suspect. Still, the weakness of her voice moves me. I enter the garden. "What's the matter?"

"Excuse my boldness, but I am in need of immediate aid."

I take a few hesitant steps toward the bush. And now I see: The basket of fruits and cucumbers lies toppled on the ground. One fig has split, its numerous seeds wet and naked to the air, pungent. My nostrils prickle. My senses are heightened, as during the fasting of Ramadhan. This must be the servant girl I passed on my way to the mosque. I hurry around the roses.

She sits with her knees pulled to her chest and her face tucked under. "Don't look upon me, please, kind sir. My clothes are ripped. My *chador* is gone."

I go down on one knee beside her. "Are you hurt?"

She doesn't answer. The pins that held her hair up have come away. Braids hang down her back, all the way to the ground. Between them I see smooth, dark skin. Her clothes have been reduced to rags.

"I'll find Ayeh." Ayeh is the head of the women servants; this girl is her charge. "I'll send her to help you."

"No." The girl tilts her head up just enough so that

I see her frightened eyes. "Please don't leave me like this. What if he comes again?"

Now the scene makes sense. Of course I cannot leave her alone. "What animal attacked you?" I peer around at the bushes, from which the savage beast might still be watching.

"None," she says. "It was a man."

Anger bubbles up from my stomach, souring my mouth. "Who? Who did this to you?"

"No one would believe me."

"I will. Tell me."

She whispers, but so softly, I cannot catch the name.

I put my ear close to her mouth.

She falls against me, and my hands catch her instinctively. Now her arms circle my neck, and her face nuzzles in the hollow of my throat. "Carry me to safety."

I have never touched an adult woman who was not in my family. My arms burn with energy. "Who?" My voice catches on the single word.

"Who?" she echoes, her lips moving against my neck. "Do you mean who am I?"

I had meant who was her attacker, but now I can see that I should have had compassion for the victim, not just rage for the criminal. Shame reduces me, makes me compliant. I stand, holding her in my arms like a small child. "Who are you?" I say as gently as I can.

"Zanejadu," she breathes. Her breath is roses. Her voice is harps. Her name is familiar.

Zanejadu.

I look down at this woman curled against my chest and try to place her name.

She sighs and arches slightly.

I glimpse the curve of her breast, a hint of black. My head feels light. I cannot think straight, I cannot take my eyes from her flesh. This is the effect of fasting, I'm sure. The skin of her hand on my neck is thick as rose flesh — as *gule sourkh.* This is dream.

But the pulse in my temples is loud and real. Temptation must be fought. I should pray, but I cannot even make the *rakatha,* for I cannot put down this unfortunate woman.

Where is my faith? Oh, that the basic principles should recount themselves, permeating my being.

Nothing enters my head.

My groin throbs.

Let me find that rage that consumed me only moments ago. "Who did this to you?"

"Orasmyn," she whispers. "The prince."

"I am Orasmyn," I say stupidly.

She is kissing my neck. "You did this. You."

"I did what, Zanejadu?" Zanejadu! The sorceress *pari* who tried to seduce the heroes Isfandiyar and Rustam. I drop her. "Wicked *pari,* you would trap me now."

"Foolish prince," she says with a sneer, "you are already trapped."

"I'll get free."

"With your father's plan?"

Did she follow me to the mosque? Was she perhaps one of the ants feeding on the dead scorpion, listening as we talked? "It is my plan, not Father's, and it will work."

"Proud, stupid Orasmyn. Jumail was a she-camel. Only a woman's love can undo the curse. And no woman will ever love you."

"My mother loves me."

The *pari* laughs and gives a little yank to my beard. "You know the love I mean. Your skin trembled under my kiss."

I turn and run. Rose thorns stab through my feet, but I run fast. I look over my shoulder. She is gone, vision of iniquity, yet she lingers, she coats me. I run as though for my life, I run, and . . .

SLAM.

PART 2

Strange Life

CHAPTER FIVE

Blood

Something crawls across my cheek. Delicate. It hesitates, then crawls again. I feel it lightly, strangely, as though it walks from hair to hair. Six legs. How extraordinary, that I can detect six legs. It crawls toward my open mouth. I jerk my head.

That didn't feel right. My head is heavy. A huge, doughy lump.

The insect is gone. I open my eyes. Clouds thinly veil the moon. Slowly the form of leaves darkens against the night air. I am outside. The perfume in the air tells all: I am in the rose garden.

Memory strains, but no recollection comes. Only the sense that I shouldn't be here, a vague worry I cannot understand.

My skin crawls as though I'm blanketed in insects.

I roll onto my stomach. My whole body is heavy.

Exhaustion closes my eyes. It makes no sense to fight it. The servants will come looking for me soon enough.

I surrender myself to sleep.

A crow caws loudly. A crow's caw is a prayer to the Merciful One.

I open my eyes to the haze of predawn. Dawn comes! Soon the *imam*'s helper will call out the *adhan* for morning prayer. Memory returns like a desert wind that would steal the breath from every living creature. Everyone in the palace will rise for prayer. Father will rise. I must get to my room and lock myself in.

Or this will be the day that I die.

I lift my head to look around, and fall with its weight onto my back. I rise to my shoulder.

Horror! The body of a lion stretches out before me. The beast has made it over the high wall of the hunting park.

I open my mouth to scream, but swallow the scream just in time.

For this must be the *pari*'s curse! If I call out, Father will come with bow and arrow, and the lion will leap away as the arrow enters my heart. Clever, cruel curse.

Breath whistles in my nostrils.

I jump to my feet. But I'm heavy. My head stays

low. This is not my balance. This is not my weight. Nothing is right. I am ill. Over my shoulder I see the back and tail of the lion. I try to run. I fall, splayed on the packed earth under a hazelnut tree.

In panic I turn to face the beast that will tear my throat.

Nothing's there.

I look down. The massive paw of the beast waits on the ground directly below me. Does it tease me? Ardeshir talked about lions yesterday. He said lions rest or hunt or copulate. He said nothing of teasing their prey—or, at least, not within my earshot.

Has the *pari* taken on the form of this lion? Does she wait only to increase the torture? What else could explain why the beast doesn't lunge at such close range?

Impossible close range. Nothing is right.

Can I outwit a master hunter? I inch my right foot forward.

The lion's paw moves the slightest bit.

A wretched idea begins to form—more wretched than anything I have ever heard or read about.

I look down at the lion's left paw.

I move my left foot.

The lion's left paw moves.

Oh, evil thought! I lift my left foot.

The lion's left paw lifts.

This cannot be. The *pari* has bewitched me again, so that now I believe I am lion. I put my mouth over my foreleg and clamp down. Hair mats against my tongue and palate. My leg hurts; I taste my own blood.

I am insane.

My eyes flicker all about in fear. This is too close to people.

A lion's thought. My thought.

I walk on unsteady legs. I try to visualize four-legged animals—a cat, a dog, a deer. Right front paw, left rear paw. Left front paw, right rear paw.

I walk carefully, gradually increasing my pace. After a while I can do this without thought. I can walk a lion's walk; crazy or not, I can do this.

My skin is loose. It's as though I walk inside it, my muscles rippling beneath a coat. I stop at a coconut tree and spread my claws in wonder. Then I retract them and walk.

A lion's walk. A lion's body.

Last night the woman in my arms was but a crude dream compared to the nightmare of this morning. I yell to wake myself, to return to my sensibilities. A roar thunders within my head.

Shouts come from the palace. They scream of lions.

I am lion! No insanity, no nightmare, truth. And the hunt starts within the hour.

"The lion's in the rose garden—there! Get your swords!"

I run in a circle. Where can I go? The town is not safe; people will be coming at me from every side. Every side except the hunting park. And that's exactly where the *pari* wants me to go—to the woods, where my father will hunt me down. The brilliance of the way this *pari* carries out her curse takes my breath away.

I need a plan. In this moment more than any previous of my entire life, I need to think straight. I am Orasmyn, the scholar prince; I can figure out an escape.

The smell of incense on the clothing of people disgusts me. The stink of their sweat sickens me, panics me. They are coming. They will kill me.

I'm loping now to the gate of the hunting park, fighting the urge to break into a full run for fear that I'll stumble in this awkward body. People cry out from behind. I sense where their voices come from with a precision new to me. The gate is fastened by a rope loop. I put my front paws on the top and lift the loop with my teeth. And I am in the park. Nothing can hold me back any longer—I run at breakneck speed.

Past elm, oak, and maple, without thought, running, running. I skirt around the chinar, poplar, and magnolia. I run like the maddened. The trees change to mainly pine and spruce—trees that signal I am nearing the foot of the mountains.

I stop at last. The world seems to keep rushing by for a few seconds—then it gradually settles. This part of the hunting park is unfamiliar. I listen: The only noises beyond my panting are those of animals.

I pant. Me. My long, wide tongue hangs from my mouth, cooling my whole body. This is me, this is Orasmyn, panting.

The sun climbs; it is full morning. My stomach contracts painfully—I am famished. Reason tells me to find a good hiding place and stay there. Stay until this spell passes. Because it has to pass. I will not allow myself to believe it can last. Terror can undo a mind; terror can lead to irreparable mistakes. I will hide and wait out this spell.

Yet I feel like an empty olive oil barrel. I need filling. And lions are fast. This much I just learned. I can race away at the first sign of danger.

Birds catch my attention. Small dark gray birds with black masks at the eyes. I've seen these birds all my life, but I've never paid attention to them. A larger gray bird with a white belly lands on a branch high above the flock of small birds. A pair of charcoal gray birds preen one another on a low branch.

Gray and black and white.

The leaves range from light gray to black.

The trunk of the plane tree they sit in is dark gray.

My own fur is the lightest gray.

I see no colors on earth.

Yet the sky is blue.

My eyes are drawn back to the birds. To their quick and bright black eyes. This feline eyesight that is so impoverished of color is keen with respect to distance, for I detect each feather of the birds clearly, each small flutter.

I would eat the entire flock.

Raw. Filled with forbidden blood. That is something to think about. But not now. Not while hunger rules me.

I leap to a low branch, teeter for a moment, and drop clumsily to the other side.

I leap again, this time taking a few steps along the branch to find my balance. But as soon as I stop moving, I fall off.

I circle the tree. I must get up there. It's not the birds that urge me on at this point. The flock took to the air at my first leap. No, it's the thought of the *taziyan* — the greyhounds — and the elephants — Kooma and the two others I have not seen. Somehow this thought has come to me right now — and it prevails over my hunger. The dogs and elephants will come to drive the wild cats toward the hunters. The ground is not safe.

I leap again, from one branch to a higher one, to an even higher one, and flop down immediately, straddling the limb. The weight of my hanging legs jars me. A knob of wood presses sharp against my belly. I scooch forward and suddenly fall to my right, hugging the branch tight so that I dangle upside down. Nausea fills me. The first time I climbed on a camel's back, I felt sick like this. It was a gigantic creature, from Bactria. Heights are not my strong point. But I cannot hang here forever.

I drop, twisting in midair, whipping my tail around instinctively, but not fast enough. I land on one side and scramble to my feet.

My stomach contracts again.

Hide or hunt?

The lion in me preempts the man. I must eat.

My ears stand stiff. My back goes rigid. Something watches me. Something that smells totally new—a strong musk. My peripheral vision, which is keen indeed, cannot capture this something. I turn my head slowly, slowly.

The lioness is perfectly still. Her shoulders and hips protrude, as though the rest of her hangs from that frame. She stares at me. Now she stretches her neck forward, and her torso seems to pull together, firm and high on the bone, as though she's gathering energy. She gives a low, sad moan.

I bolt. I run in as straight a path as the trees allow. So many trees, but nowhere to hide. O Merciful One, let me find a prince's energy. My legs must go faster. I run.

A new lioness gets to her feet in front of me, as though forming from the dirt itself.

I swerve, skid, stumble, and roll.

The lioness who has been following me is far behind. She trots up slowly, in no rush.

I stand and face her. I am lion, I am lion, I am lion. I've never heard if lions are cannibals, but if they aren't, O Merciful One, let me remember I am lion.

The other lioness stays in her spot, ears cocked, eyes wide, lips closed. She watches intently.

The first lioness slows to a walk. Her lips are black; her nose is black and riddled with scars. She makes puffs at regular intervals through those lips and nostrils. She stops a body's length from me. Large whiskers form parallel horizontal rows on her cheeks, each emerging from a small dark spot. The top row has only spots, no whiskers. Her face is wide—over wide jaws.

I think I will pass out.

She blinks and looks away. The back rim of her small, rounded ears is black. Her right ear has two nicks.

I hear myself panting.

The lioness looks at me again. Her deep-set eyes have round pupils, not vertical slits like the pupils of the bazaar cats. The black tuft on the end of her tail swats across her rear. She opens her mouth fully and holds it there.

I count four fangs and four knife-edged teeth behind them, then molars. I am dead unless I attack

first. I crouch, praying that my body will know how
to spring.

Ahchoo! The lioness snaps her jaw shut.

She sneezed. That lioness sneezed.

She squats and sits like the Sphinx I visited on my
pilgrimage to Mecca. She looks away again.

I stay taut, as ready as my queasy heart allows.

The second lioness trots over now. She comes right
up to where I crouch in the dirt. I am panting so hard,
I think my heart will explode. She rubs that part of
her head right above the eye against my cheek. She
puts her weight into the rub; it's all I can do to keep
from falling to the other side. She crouches now, and
pushes her head along the length of my whole body,
until we are rubbing, side against side. Suddenly she
springs up and twirls around to put her face near
mine again. She licks my head. My neck. Her tongue
is long and rough, and the whole time she is softly
humming.

The first lioness watches, her gaze open.

I pant more loudly, but the dizziness has passed. A
new feeling enters me—a rush like waters cascading at
the first spring thaw in these mountains. It invigorates.

The second lioness rolls onto her back, exposing
white fur. She waits expectantly.

I know what she waits for. And I have no idea how
to give it. This is me, inside this body, this is me,

Orasmyn. How can I think of responding to this lioness? But I am not thinking. I pant.

She gets to her feet and trots around me, her tail raised.

I find myself on my feet. I trot after her.

She stops and crouches.

I stand behind her.

She lifts her tail higher, her flanks higher.

I am hot with the impulse to mate. I look back at the first lioness. She looks at me, then away.

I straddle the lioness at my feet, my front legs straight on either side of her ribcage, my back legs flexed. A quiet rumble comes from her throat. I have the urge to bite the back of her neck, but I resist with all my might. Instead, I bite at the air. But I cannot resist other urges. I thrust, and within seconds she yowls and twists under me, swatting at my head.

I duck to the side, and she's out from under me in an instant. I jump around to face her, confused, ready to defend myself.

Instead, she drops onto her side with a sigh.

I wait.

She doesn't even look at me. She lolls her head onto the ground and breathes loudly.

Slowly I lower myself till I lie beside her, ever wary of those paws that can swat.

The weight of my body pulls at me. I let my head fall

to the ground. Everything about me is strange. But the way the ground welcomes this huge body of mine feels more natural than any bedroom I've slept in.

We stay lying that way for several minutes. Perhaps a quarter of an hour. And now the first lioness walks in front of me, presenting her rear.

My chest tightens. I find her the most sexually arousing female I have ever imagined. The rumble in her throat lures me. This time my fangs clamp down on her neck without hesitation. I do not break her skin, yet I feel her tremble under me. The trembling excites me more—me, the prince who never joined the hunt—I am excited by the fear of the female below me. We mate, and I jump off immediately afterward.

All three of us lie in a beam of sunlight, resting.

I try to think. I am Orasmyn. I have a conscience and a soul. I am Orasmyn.

Hunger returns, banishing thought. A low growl comes unbidden from my throat.

Both females rise as one. They trot away.

I feel stupid. It is insanely dangerous to stay with them. Yet the idea of being alone in lion form undoes me. I follow them.

We travel one behind the other, slowly and silently.

The first female falls to the ground in a crouch. The second female follows suit. She looks over her shoulder at me. I crouch.

The first female creeps forward, her chest close to the ground.

The second female trots in a half crouch over to the side and out of sight.

I don't know who to follow. I don't understand what's going on. I stay put.

The stag somehow got separated from the herd. He feeds on grasses that have managed to grow tall in a small clearing. He hasn't spotted us. His breath moves with a light rasp. I can hear it from where I crouch. Even with his head down, it's easy to see this is a tall animal. Upright and reaching for the highest leaves, his antlers probably stand taller than the tallest man. The tines are so many, I'd have to concentrate to count them. And each antler ends in a triple point. He must be young—maybe even a hart—for otherwise he would have dropped those antlers by now and new, fuzzy ones would be growing.

A breeze ripples my fur, plays with the hair on the tips of the first lioness's ear. I stare at the two nicks. They charm me. They make her seem vulnerable.

Did she move? If so, it was almost imperceptible. Now again. She makes her way forward a finger's length at a time, ever more flattened against the ground. I watch. In the span of a half hour, she moves no more than the width of the small pool in the fruit-tree garden. The very tip of her tail twitches.

The deer jumps to attention. He has caught our scent. How stupid of us to approach upwind of the prey. He leaps away.

The second female comes out in front of him, running full speed.

The stag stops, bewildered. He leaps to the side.

The first female dashes out. Her claws grab at the stag's rump. Within seconds, he's on his side. He struggles to get up, kicks her fiercely in the face, lets out a bleat. The second female bites his throat. The stag thrashes, goes limp.

The lionesses tear open the stag from belly to anus. They drag out the viscera, scooping with their paws, pulling with those fangs. One is chewing at the organs while the other chomps into the flesh at the groin. I watch, fascinated. The lioness with the nicked ear, my lioness, dislocates a hind leg at the pelvis and drags it aside to gnaw on.

They growl as they eat. The growls entice me. I stand and walk to my lioness. She looks up at me. Hesitantly, I reach my head forward to the meat. She springs away in alarm and goes back to the carcass. The other lioness growls louder at her. My lioness rips a foreleg from the shoulder and drags it into the bushes. She flops down and eats.

I am still standing over the half-chewed hind leg. Both females look at me between bites. The scent of blood dampens the air. A tiny spasm of thought far back in my brain warns me. But it is too distant to understand, like a memory from infancy, before I could talk. A growl eases from my throat. I crouch and eat.

Hot blood fills my mouth, coats my tongue thickly; its aroma invades my nostrils, replacing all other smells. This flesh is wonderful.

I finish the leg and walk over to the carcass.

The other lioness jumps aside for me. I take the remaining hind leg and pull at it until the femur snaps away from the hip socket and black blood spurts up in my face. I eat this leg.

Both females are now ripping at the shoulder of the carcass. We eat.

Finally, I stop. The lionesses have stopped, as well. The head of the stag lies far from its ribcage. The grasses are wet with blood.

My belly is bloated and swollen, as are those of the females. We have eaten enough meat to feed a whole town. Meat and gristle and hide. We gorged.

The lionesses lick away the blood from their chops. Then they lick their paws and rub their faces against the moist paws. Grooming is slow and luxurious. Finally, they rise and I follow them. They are strangers to this hunting park, yet they seem to know exactly where they're going.

I walk naturally, my hind paws landing in the precise spots my front paws have just vacated. My ears turn to catch sounds from every direction. My tail swings. Managing this body requires not thought, but surrender. It is as though the muscles govern themselves.

We come to a stream. I know this stream; I have splashed up and down its length on hot summer days. I splashed without fear—for these woods held no predators large enough to threaten me. No predators large enough to threaten that stag. That must have been why he was such an easy prey; he never expected death.

The lionesses lower their front legs and lap water. They move in a companionable synchrony, and I sense they are sisters, perhaps even twins. I crouch and lap. The water is delicious.

We trot through the trees. My lioness stops to defecate. She leaves the steaming liquid pile and trots on. I am drawn to it. I smell it, then follow her.

We stop in a thicket and sink to the ground, emitting hoarse puffs of air. My lioness looks at me with a steady, open gaze. Her eyes accept the death of the stag and the hard earth and everything; they accept me. She licks my muzzle, humming all the while. I see now that she suffered a deep gash in her nose from the stag's hoof. It was hidden before under the blood from the meat. I lick her wound. She rubs her cheek and ear against mine, sighs, and lets herself fall onto her back with her legs flopping in the air. Within moments both lionesses sleep.

I watch them as though in a trance.

Slowly my mind comes awake.

I know what I have done this morning. The sense of conscious realization that characterized Orasmyn's thoughts, the sense that has eluded me since I woke, has finally returned. I know what I have done. All without the *wudhu* that clenses body and soul first. All without prayer. And so much blood.

Father would never eat blood. Mother would never eat blood. All meat must be properly bled. But my people, the people of great Persia, have eaten blood since long before Islam came to this land, since ancient times. The townspeople saved the camel and sheep blood from the sacrifice yesterday. I know they did. We all know. They ate it later, congealed and cut into cubes. We *hajjiha* even watched as the women dipped cotton in the blood. We knew they brought it home to dry. When a child is sick, they will put the blood-hardened cotton in water and feed the child the water with a spoon. We knew this. Everyone knows.

Perhaps it is my Persian heritage that allowed me to eat the blood of the stag. Eat without the ritual prayers first. Eat ravenously until I was obscenely oversatiated.

I listen to the grunts of the lionesses as they sleep. I hear their heartbeats. I hear their heartbeats!

No, I didn't eat blood because of my Zoroastrian heritage. I ate blood because I am lion.

I mated with lionesses.

O Merciful One, the mix of good and evil that the *Qur'an* speaks of has tipped within me.

I await my slaughter.

CHAPTER SIX

Birds

The earth vibrates. The lionesses jump to their feet. They race off. I chase after.

I stop.

It's the elephants—I know this simply from the sound. Dogs bark. They are still far away, but they're moving. They come from the direction of the mountains. Abdullah and the other *mahout*s must have led them there early this morning.

If I follow the lionesses, we will be driven toward the hunters. Father will kill me. Perhaps with his bare hands.

Did I not sit here waiting for death?

But that was another me. The lion me lives.

I lope back to the stream and splash into the center. It's deep, and I slap wildly at the water with my forepaws. I'm swimming now, a sort of random paddling with all legs at once. At places the stream is shallow, and my paws run along the bottom. I'm going with the current, back toward the palace. But the other direction, upstream, leads toward Kooma and the dogs.

The thought of the dogs spurs me on. I have never been afraid of dogs, yet now I am panic stricken. Yapping dogs.

I need a plan; this body cannot simply trust every compulsion that assails it. As long as I stay in the stream, no dogs can follow my scent, at least. So maybe my lion self made a good choice when it jumped into the water. But I'm getting closer to the palace fast—the water follows a straighter path than I did when I was running through the woods. I see a line of cypresses not far off, and I know they flank the path back to the entrance gate of the hunting park.

It's hard to hear anything else above the noise of the water. I cannot know if the hunters' horses are gathered at the entrance to the hunting park or if they have already begun to move toward the prey.

The stream has narrowed and grown shallow. I walk in the center, the water not quite up to my chest. Now the wall that separates the hunting park from the palace grounds comes into view. A small bridge spans the stream ahead.

I must make a choice. I move to the very edge of

the stream and crouch. If I stay on this side of the wall, I can try to slink along unseen until I reach the gate. Then I can make a dash for it.

For what?

My room is no haven. Besides, I could never open the doors.

The *pari* said Father would kill me today. If midnight comes and I am still alive, perhaps the spell will be broken. All I have to do is live until midnight. There must be a place I can hide.

I walk out of the stream and close to the wall. Water drips from my fur with small pluds on the earth. My panting is so loud, I shut my jaw fast and almost choke on my tongue.

A man talks on the other side of the wall. Kiyumars. He speaks of preparations for the midday meal, which will be very soon. They are making *halim bademjan*—lamb with eggplant and onions—and *fessenjan ba morgh ya goosht*—chicken in walnut-onion-pomegranate sauce. These are meals fit for guests, tender and succulent. I imagine the hunting party eating these foods that took the entire morning to prepare, then placing a lump of sugar on their tongues and sipping aromatic tea through it. Their meal will be nothing like the meal I shared with the lionesses. The blood has washed off my paws, but it may well still stain my face.

A woman answers Kiyumars. It is Roya, my mother's own maidservant. All the servants have been enlisted to help in meals because there are so many guests here for the hunt.

Would Kiyumars recognize his friend in me? Would he help hide me?

A ridiculous thought.

I remember the fear in Kiyumars' eyes as he came to find me yesterday and warn me not to go off walking because of the lions and tigers.

I walk farther, my side grazing the wall. Birds scream as I pass a bush. A small flock flies into a date palm.

"Who's there?" Kiyumars calls from the other side of the wall.

Can't birds take flight without questioning? How annoying Kiyumars can be.

But I understand: Kiyumars worries that a guest has lost his way. He's giving Roya instructions and hurrying ahead to the gate. He will come through in a moment. He will see me.

I race back to the water. I crouch and go under the bridge, my face half in the water, my distended belly touching the streambed. I'm past the wall now. Roya's back is turned to me. She walks toward the palace. Who else is about?

"Is someone there?" calls Kiyumars. I pinpoint his

voice: He's standing on the inside of the wall, at the edge of the stream, just a few paces from the bridge.

Stupid birds, who endangered me so.

Birds. That's it. I slouch out of the water and make a dash for the fat, round tower where the pigeons live. The sides are speckled with openings in the stones, perches for the birds. There's a door at the bottom so that servants can scoop out the droppings and spread them as fertilizer on the melon beds. Perhaps a thousand pigeons call this tower home. The door is closed, but not latched. I dig at its bottom edge with my claws. It comes open. I go inside and work my paw under the door to pull it closed. It swings open again. I need to wedge it in place.

My paws have sunk to the ankle in pigeon droppings. Someone must have scooped out the bottom within the past week, for I've seen the droppings much deeper than this before. The pungent, unpleasant scent makes me woozy. I scrape one forepaw through the muck to form a little wall at the door opening. Now I pull the door shut again and work my paw out from underneath. The door stays, sealed by the muck.

Did anyone see me?

No one screamed. No one shouted.

But even if no one saw me enter the tower, I must have left paw prints. The dirt is dry and hard, but my paws were sopping wet from the stream. O Merciful One, bring a wind. Dry my prints. Blow them away. Be merciful.

The pigeons coo nervously from their perches above me. But they don't take to the air. Pigeons are placid, thanks be to the Merciful One.

I yawn, though I'm not tired. And I stretch. First, with all four paws close together, my head down, and my back with its midpoint high. Next, with my front paws stretched forward, my shoulders low, my rump high, and my back arched with my belly close to the ground. My claws extend, and the muck enters between my toes. The stretches leave me feeling absurdly, unreasonably calm.

I drop to my side, rest my chin on my crossed front paws, and sleep.

CHAPTER SEVEN

Death

The *adhan* for the morning prayers wakes me. For
a second I'm lost in the hot dark, then I remember where I am. I lift a hand. Though I cannot see, I
know immediately from the weight: It is not hand,
but paw.

I am still lion; the *pari*'s curse endures, though a
full day passed.

The realization neither shocks nor saddens me.
This is simply fact. I drift in and out of sleep.

Pigeons are smelly. I am smelly, smeared with their
droppings. I snort to clear my nose, but the same
odor reenters.

On and off all day, voices come. The servants. The
hunters. The *imam* and his helper on the way to the
mosque. Many pass by the pigeon tower, but no one
stops. People must be searching for me, but I cannot

make out what anyone says. The pigeons keep up a continuous muffled din of stupid warbles.

I hear the *adhan* for the noon prayers, the afternoon prayers, the sunset prayers, and the night prayers. Between the calls, I sleep. There is a strange solidity to my sleep, as though nothing can truly bother me. Almost a drugged sleep, like when I was a child and my nursemaid Ava had me drink thick, sticky liquids that tasted awful but numbed me for days. There is also a timelessness to my sleep. Were it not for the *adhan,* here in the darkness of the tower I'd have no sense of time passing. And I wouldn't care. Perhaps I am fundamentally lazy.

Or perhaps digesting this much meat takes too much blood from my brain, so that I can't do much else.

One thing I know by nightfall, though, is that I must leave the tower. My mouth is dry as uncooked rice. Thirst compels me.

I stand up. Pigeon droppings fall from my fur in clumps. It is good to be on all fours. I stretch again, long long. This body brings unexpected pleasures—a simple stretch becomes a languorous moment.

I lean against the wooden door. It resists briefly, then pops open, swinging wide. I crouch as low as I can and creep out. No one is about. I lick the muck from my paws, front and hind—this time, I won't leave a trail.

I stand upright so that I can move with more ease. The night air still smells of the evening meal—cooked meat. It stirs no interest in me. I wonder if I will ever be hungry again.

The air also smells of humans. My muscles contract under my skin. Fear presses me to run.

But there's one more smell. A musky odor that confuses me with longing and unexplained dread. It comes from the men's pavilion.

I trot, ears alert, eyes continuously scanning the palace, the bushes, all the grounds. The pavilion's marble floor is cold under my thick, spongy pads. I feel uncertain, as though I'll slip, legs splayed to either side. I want to get away.

But that odor pulls me on.

She lies in the center of the floor. Her tail stretches out straight as an arrow. Her chest is pocked with holes. Dried blood mats her fur. It's dark, and I don't see as well as in daylight, but I recognize the sound and smell of death. I put my face to hers, and the flies disperse. My tongue runs along her jaw, up to her ear. To the two nicks.

My lioness.

She seems so much smaller in death, as though she shrinks. She seems delicate. And piercingly lonely.

Lions are cannibals, I know this now, for a part of me accepts this body as meat.

But another part of me moans the loss of a female—of this female—whom I realize I would have followed day after day had the elephants not come.

I am stupid with grief. I lie on the floor beside her. Insects move from her body to mine and back. Their wings go hush hush. The night air stings my open eyes. Finally, I shut them and sleep.

The footsteps belong to a man. He approaches the pavilion from the palace side. The body of the lioness lies between me and him. I know this man. Perhaps the *pari* guides the feet of the Shah, for it is not yet dawn and he carries no lantern—he can make out less in the dark than I can, I'm sure.

I see my lioness running for her life, then turning to face her tormenters—turning to face the Shah. But her jaws were more ferocious than he had imagined. So the arrows flew as she lunged at him. Arrows from his companions as well as from the Shah. My brave, lost lioness.

The Shah missed his chance to fulfill his destiny as ruler of all Persia—to kill a lion with his bare hands.

It is well past midnight of the second day since I found myself in lion form. The spell is strong. I remember the *pari* Zanejadu, her laugh, her words; only a woman's love can undo this terror.

No woman will ever love me.

The *pari* has won.

Yet, in a sense, it is I who won, for I am still alive.

The Shah's bare feet slap quietly on the marble. The insects investigate him; he swats with one hand, but still comes closer. He kneels beside my lioness.

I stand.

The Shah gasps loudly. His hands fly up beside his face. His mouth hangs open, as though he's shrieking silently.

I lower my head, offer my neck to his bare hands.

He doesn't move.

Nor do I.

He has stopped breathing. But now he takes in breath again and lowers one hand ever so slowly to rest it on the top of my head.

I wait.

"Master, is that you?" It is Shahpour's voice. He's running toward us. "What . . . ? Lion!" he shouts and runs back toward the palace.

The Shah's breath comes fast, in little bursts. "Beast," he whispers. "Why? Why have you come?" He smells of pistachio, his favorite nut. He smells human, familiar, father, meat.

Loud voices come from the palace. I see torches.

Father puts his hands around my throat, reaching under my thick mane.

The men are coming.

Father's hands tighten.

And now I see the *pari*'s curse realizing itself—I see the Shah standing over the body of Prince Orasmyn, looking at his own hands aghast. A father who has killed his son. An excruciating pain that can never lessen.

I butt him hard in the chest.

Father falls backward.

I run.

The men with torches are in the pavilion; they surround Father. Two brave souls peer out into the dark after me. But I am already past their line of vision, and no one dares chase a lion by night.

I run to the fruit-tree garden. The small pool shines black in the dimmest moonlight. I bend my forelegs and drink. I drink and drink until I slake this thirst.

If only the face of the *pari* would appear in the water, I'd drink it away. I'd obliterate it for all eternity.

I walk back toward the palace. The voices have died down; most of the men have gone back to bed. But three men with torches guard the body of my lioness.

I stay close to the wall of the hunting park, completely obscured in the dark, and go to the fragrance garden. I walk through *sewti*, which blooms white year round, especially toward the end of the rains. I walk through *mongra*, a yellow I will never again distinguish from gray. *Bholsari* and *chambeli* and *riabel* and *kuzah*. All the flowers I have tended with care, working alongside the *baghbanha*—the gardeners— alongside Kiyumars. I roll around the *gulhaye sourkh*— my dear, dear rosebeds—aching for the loss of so much, of everything gentle, everything good.

Yes, the *pari*'s curse meant precisely this. For this is death, is it not? A lion may be the one beast that could never survive on the Shah's grounds— the grounds of the ruler of all Persia. He would always be hunting me down. The lion is banished. My father has killed his son.

I gather myself within this strange new skin and trot off to the north, along the path that leads forever to the mountains.

PART 3

Lion

CHAPTER EIGHT

Alone

By full dawn I am in the mountains. Wilderness lies to the north—a great wilderness to hide me.

I need a plan—I need to gather my energies and forge ahead. I tell myself these things, yet I have no urge to act upon that knowledge; nothing perturbs me. My belly is still full. The world slows. For now I nap, basking in the open sunshine, far from any path humans might take, but close to water.

When I wake, I check my hands again—they are still paws. I knew they would be; by now I knew. I roll in the stream, then rise and crouch, rise and crouch, growling softly, thinking the words:

> In the name of God, Most Compassionate,
>   Most Merciful.
> Praise be to God, Lord of the Worlds.

This bathing is my attempt at the *wudhu;* this growl, my attempt at prayer, pathetic though it be. I wonder how long it will take before I forget the words to *Al-Fatiha,* the opening of the *Qur'an.* May I not live that long.

I spend hours intently watching other animals: birds, insects, lizards, and snakes. The day lengthens.

But night, when it finally comes to the mountain, comes all at once, in a hurry, carrying unfamiliar noises that press upon my isolation. All of me longs for company, the comfort of community. I wander silently, alert for dangers, searching until I find a protected ledge. The rock is warm under my belly. After awhile, I sleep.

The sound of scampering feet wakes me. My eyes adjust quickly to the night. A young hyrax runs across my ledge. It darts, rodentlike, to the low bush on the other side and feeds, oblivious of me. Five more young come racing after it, chasing each other in glee. They are no larger than my paw.

I lift my head to watch better.

Two of the creatures notice me. The hairs on their backs near their scent glands rise, creating a light spot. I stay perfectly still, and they return to feeding and intermittent playing.

Now two adults come along, the size of rabbits. Their pelts are thick. I wonder how they manage in this summer heat. My own hair is shorter and thinner than theirs by far. One of the adults sees me and stops. It waits, chin whiskers twitching. Then it comes several steps closer and stops again.

Its curiosity delights me. But a sense of mischief enters me. I roar. The hyrax practically flips over itself backward and disappears. My roar grows as my mouth opens wider. It lasts a good thirty or forty seconds, rocking me sideways. When my jaw finally shuts, there is no trace of animal nearby. I would laugh if I could.

That roar was powerful and majestic—and exceedingly loud. It carried far. I get to my feet and climb higher into the mountains. I don't stop until morning.

Days pass. Sleep alternates with short, erratic meanderings. The only consistency to my day is immersion in mountain pools at dawn and dusk followed by prayer, such as it is, and long drinks. No thirst I ever had as a human compares with my leonine thirst.

Hunger finally comes again—and with it, ever-clearer thoughts. I try my luck at catching lizards; my luck is nonexistent. One day. Another. I look around and realize my hunger has led me back down to the foothills, where the game is more plentiful. Yet still I catch nothing.

By daylight I hurry along, my head upright and high, my ears cocked forward. All my senses sharpen, as they do when I fast during Ramadhan. But I am not light-headed, as I am then. I am tight and ready. I am hungry.

And I am a dreadfully poor hunter.

I can hardly sleep anymore. I roll in water and pray and wander, disoriented.

Think, Orasmyn.

I stop, sit on my haunches, and watch.

After a few hours, I see a large black bird rise to the sky. A second follows. Vultures. I am already trotting toward the spot they took off from. It takes a half hour to get there. The carcass of the mongoose has been ripped open. It's a big one. Its bloody flesh glistens. My mouth drools for that flesh.

A jackal slinks out of the bushes far ahead of me, close to the mongoose, tail bushy, stripes pale. Then three more. They rush at the carcass, which is barely enough for a small meal for me.

I growl deep in my throat.

The jackals face me in surprise. I remember how my lioness hunted upwind of the stag—how her strategy depended solely on sight and sound. Now these jackals have failed to even use sight—for they should have looked back over their shoulders before leaving the safety of the bush.

But, then, they never expected a lion.

They stand in a row, and one lets out a long, wavering howl. The others join, repeating four times, ending in a series of quick yelps. It's an eerie cry. If I didn't see them for myself, I would have guessed there were many more of them.

I roar.

The jackals are gone by the time my jaw closes. Only now do I realize that the instant I first saw them I should have flattened myself and crept up on them. A jackal meal would have been much more hearty than this mongoose snack.

The vultures have picked out the liver, the eyes, the entrails, but the skeletal frame is whole except for a split in the backbones, up high. I eat the flesh, cracking the bones and swallowing everything that will go down. The mongoose's distended stomach remains intact. I rip it open with a claw. A barely digested snake curls there.

I eat the snake, the stomach, the pointed head and long tail and grizzled fur of the mongoose, and reflect upon the probable drama. The mongoose surprised the snake. Then somehow it managed to break its own neck. Perhaps the snake had a part in it—causing indigestion with a toxin, or simply making the animal clumsy around its full belly. The vultures discovered the dead mongoose. And the jackals waited for the vultures to finish. Their fearsome howl is deceptive, if that's the case: for they are not bold. Then came the lion.

The snake, the mongoose, the vultures, the jackals, me—all caught in an endless cycle of bloodied jaws and claws.

But at least the lion has the respite afforded by a distended belly after a gargantuan meal. If only I can learn to shake off the lethargy that follows a gorging, I can perhaps hold on to my human mind. I can think the thoughts of a man.

But at this moment my stomach still has room for more meat. If I see the jackals again, I will attack. I will eat jackal.

And now I realize I shouldn't have made such short work of the mongoose meal; I should have left something other than this mess of scattered teeth and bone splinters. Something to lure the jackals back.

I am inept.

And I have eaten again without the *wudhu* first, without prayer. If I had stopped to find a stream and roll in it, then pray, the jackals would have eaten all the meat. But that isn't what made me eat so quickly. No, I didn't even think of that when I ate. I simply ate. There was food; I was hungry.

The lion in me prevails not only over body, but over spirit. I fool myself to hope otherwise.

I walk to the bush the jackals were hiding under before and nestle in. I sleep.

When I wake, it's night, and an edginess makes me jump to my feet. I peer through the dark. Nothing's watching me, yet somehow I am certain I have to get moving.

I trot quickly. After a few hours the wild yields to trees arranged in orderly rows with aromatic shrubs in between. A garden. One of mine. The palace itself is quiet, but voices come from the holding pen. It is suicidal to be here—but I am drawn forward. Night cloaks me, at least. I stay close to the wall along the hunting park, every part of me at the ready. My mind possesses a clarity of thought I have not had since I woke that first night in lion form. The closer I get to the human trappings from my old life, the more acute that clarity grows. Near the little bridge I crouch and listen.

Kiyumars' voice comes like warm rain to a dry garden. Oh, to speak with him again, to speak with my friend.

Djamchid, another servant, answers. They lament my disappearance. Kiymars scolds himself for not warning me more severely against the dangers from the wild cats brought in for the hunt. By the time the irony of his assumption hits me, the discussion has moved on to trouble with the Turks. Kiyumars overheard the Shah speak of coming war. Talk of impending bloodshed from the Turks has surrounded me my whole life. This is a real concern, but maybe not as pressing as Kiyumars thinks.

I come closer, so that I can see into the pen now. Kiyumars and Djamchid work with Abdullah and four other Indian boys. It's been a week already. Precisely a week, for the hunting guests depart at dawn.

And, oh, perhaps my human part has been working all along; perhaps it kept track of the days and brought me back here in time. For an idea forms now, an idea that shakes me to the core of my being.

I hear the *pari* Zanejadu's words again: Only a woman's love can undo the curse.

I am lion. And I will die lion, for no human woman will ever love me.

But a week ago two lionesses accepted me. And I accepted them—more than I wanted to admit.

India is lion country. India is lion country. India is lion country.

O Merciful One, forgive me. For I know I can live that life. A lion's life.

The irony of the *pari*'s curse finally hits me: The lion is king of beasts.

I stand taller to meet the challenge. I am the Prince of Persia, and I choose my destiny. I will go to India.

The departure of the Indian guests shines before me as what it truly is: an opportunity. I can follow them at a distance all the way to the wilds where lions live. I don't have to travel that great distance alone.

This is, at last, a plan. The only plan.

With the realization comes impatience. I want to begin my new life. The *pari* ruined my old life, but she cannot ruin this one. I will fight her with all my might. I will learn to enjoy the company of lions. I will take my position as king of beasts.

This thought brings another: My ears, eyes, nose all pay attention. There is no lion in the area but me. The hunters must have killed them all.

They will kill me, too, if they see me.

If I run to the southeast, the Indian caravan will pass by me in a few hours.

I rise, prepared to leave, when I notice a flicker of light from my bedroom window. I cross the open area, passing by the pavilion where the body of my lioness lay last week, and stand under the window. Two bodies breathe within, the regular breath of sleepers. I rise on my hind legs and rest my front paws on the window ledge. Lit candles line the perimeter of the room. Beside each candle are three bowls: a large one with cut roses floating in water, a medium one with smoking incense stalks standing in sand, and a small one with balls of hardened honey rolled in crushed almonds. Mother and Father lie in my bed in each other's arms. Her hair falls loose across her face; his face presses against her shoulder.

This room has become a shrine to call me back to them from whatever world I now inhabit. If I could see their beloved faces, I know they would speak of misery and of hope. Father and Mother deserve to know that I live still, though I cannot live as their son anymore.

I can never kiss them again. I can never allow myself to touch them. I cannot be Orasmyn. The loss blinds me for a moment.

When sight returns, I look back over my shoulder. There is no way to be sure that the people in the holding pen are not looking in this direction. The risk makes my upper lip curl under. I push off from my hind legs, balance for a moment with all fours on the ledge, and drop into the room.

Father groans in his sleep.

The *Shahnameh* lies on my reading platform, on the floor. With my bottom teeth, I flip open the cover. Then I use the very tip of my tongue to turn the pages. Page after page. Searching.

Father groans again and shifts, twisting his neck so that now, if his eyes open, he will see me. He will see lion.

I turn the pages faster. Finally I find the illustration I sought, the illustration I was admiring a week ago: Bahram Chubina slaying the lion-ape. I leave the book open to that page.

That's when I see the new book beside the *Shah-nameh*. It is *Gulistan — Rose Garden*. The author is Saadi. This must be the book of verse that Mother said she wanted me to read. How perfect for her to have chosen a book with the title of my beloved flower. Once upon a time, opening this book would most certainly have brought me laughter, for nothing is better than Sufi humor. Once upon a time.

Never again.

Father stirs. He is half awake.

I take the book in my mouth and spring out the window in one huge leap.

CHAPTER NINE

India

By day I trot along out of sight behind trees and bushes and the numerous boulders that lie close to the path the caravan follows. When we come to towns, the Indian travelers pass through, stocking up on foods, while I give wide berth, staying in the shadows.

I learn quickly that domesticated cats are easy prey. The lesson scared me at first, because my nursemaid Ava used to say that anyone who killed a cat would die. Dogs tied up outside houses at night are likewise easy, and that was a worse lesson—a repulsive lesson. Ava said dogs have seven souls, so they must be killed seven times to really die. If she was right, multiple souls haunt me now.

These beliefs of ancient Persia mix uneasily with the Muslim religion of my heart, yet both of them grow dearer to me with each leonine act that distances me forever.

Or maybe not forever. The book I took from the palace, *Gulistan,* lies hidden under a slab rock within the Shah's hunting park. The verses await a self that can open it and drink thirstily.

Would that such a self should survive and conquer.

But for now the self that owns me travels toward lion country, for that self quenches thirst with the blood of dogs.

The dogs must belong to Christians and Jews, since dogs are too dirty an animal for Muslims to keep. Kiyumars and I once petted a Christian dog in the bazaar when we were small. Shahpour made us bathe from head to foot before we were allowed to pray again.

The luxury of eating only tied-up animals allows me time to find water before meals and perform my version of the *wudhu* and say the prayers. Still, I fear I will never be cleansed.

After many days of winding downward through gaps and passes in the mountains, the path comes out on the great central plateau that fills much of Persia. I stand at the northwest corner of this plateau, breathing slowly in the hot, dry air. Mountain ranges extend south and east. And I know that far, far to the east another mountain range runs north to south, so that Persia is bordered by a ruggedness that suits my people.

My chest swells eagerly. The plateau holds plenty

of small game, roebucks and hares. I recognize it as my natural habitat. If I can only learn to hunt minimally well, the plateau will be welcoming.

But there is no denying that from here on, the opportunities for cover diminish. Beyond the plateau lies the even hotter desert, where, with the exception of oases—which are quite dependable—bushes and even thickets are hard to find.

I have no choice but to strike out on my own.

If I stay in the foothills and head east until I reach the mountain range that runs north-south, then follow those mountains south, I can find India for sure.

I pace. The idea of leaving the caravan irritates me and, yes, it frightens me. But it shouldn't. I am not human; these Indians are not company for me. They would kill me if they caught sight of me following them.

Or maybe they would imprison me? Maybe they would put me in one of their empty wooden lion cages and cart me to a wilderness?

I can't know.

I watch the caravan head onto the plateau, then I turn and run due east.

In the next few weeks I take to traveling mostly by night, with naps in the daytime. The pattern is difficult for me; I see somewhat better by day. But I adopt this habit for two reasons. First, the heat increases as the summer passes—and my tolerance for heat inside this hair coat is minimal. But, more important, few humans are about at night.

In the settlements nearest to the foothills, the air is heavy with the smells of traditional dishes, like *esfenaj surkh kardeh*—spinach with onions and turmeric. The vegetables don't attract me in the least, however. I eat cats and dogs. Sheep and goats would be easy prey, too, for there are abundant herds everywhere. But I know I cannot travel if I have a large meal. And I must keep traveling. If there is any promise left in my life, India holds it.

I pass nomadic tribes, women in black robes, men in flowing white with head scarves. The largest of their camels are piled high with heavy carpets, ready to be spread out on both sides of any path they cross so that passing travelers find an instant *souk*—market. I do not raid their domesticated animals—not even the rabbits. These beasts are part of their livelihood, minimal as it is; they are not mere pets. I've been told that nomads sometimes live for months on nothing but dates and camel's milk.

But there's another reason: The nomads, unlike the townspeople, might recognize the work of a lion and hunt me down.

The mountains seem never ending, even to these new eyes of mine that can see so far. Finally, after days of travel, another range cuts across them. I follow the new range southward along the eastern border of my dear Persia. Nothing is a marker of when to cross these mountains and head into India, into lion country. So I keep going south, into the searing heat.

One morning I smell the sea, the Arabian Sea of the Indian Ocean. It's time to change course. And though I would normally stretch out now for a nap, the thought of India, the hope of company at long last, precludes sleep.

The mountains are lower here than I had feared, and the trees are taller and more numerous. Everything beckons me. I travel eastward again, panting, at a quiet trot all day, stopping only to drink. I trot at night and into the next day, the next evening, a regular, mesmerizing trot. India opens to me. India. I will make this new life the best it can be.

SSSS!

A leopard.

I stop, stock-still. The air around me seems to keep moving in the rocking rhythm that cushioned me only a moment ago. My eardrums hum. I feel cut off, unreal. So unreal that fear doesn't enter. Thought forms cold and organized.

The leopard is alone and clearly taken by surprise. It stands no higher than my shoulder, with a slim, long body. It shows huge fangs.

I don't know how to fight, even if that was my inclination, which it isn't. Rather, I want to turn tail and run. But I am sure that leopard runs faster than me, especially since I've been traveling without sleep for two days. If the leopard wants a fight, there's no way to avoid it. And at least I have the benefit of size. I wait.

The air stills.

And now a rancid odor comes. The smell of fear.

The big, spotted cat springs easily into the tree beside it. It leaps from bough to bough. It stops and looks down on me. It hisses again, a warning I recognize now as defensive.

Nevertheless, I make a wide arc in my path so that I do not pass within lunging range of that cat. I run quickly, then gradually slow down to my trot.

I am lion. I may well be the fiercest predator of this land. Perhaps of any land. The fiercest predator other than humans, that is. My head extends forward. I can do this. I can be lion with no one's help. I am royal. I prowl.

Then I remember tigers. As large as lions, and faster. While the reality of the leopard somehow brought no fear, the crystal thought of a tiger brings shivers.

Fear is not my strongest feeling now, though; I am hungry. My stomach grew accustomed to my sneaky, opportunist ways on this journey: It contracted only when I saw a human settlement that I could raid. But now it's unruly, as though the encounter with the leopard has excited it. My last meal was two nights ago—a small cat, a morsel. Night will come soon. I want to eat before I find a place to sleep. I must hunt.

I stop and listen.

Before long I hear quick thuds. Hooved animals. Maybe luck is with me and some lone boy leads a goatherd through these foothills. I lope toward the sound.

Wild goats. And they spotted me before I spotted them. Or maybe they smelled me. They leap nimbly and swiftly, despite their stout bodies. I run behind, but halfheartedly, for I am sleepy and they know the terrain. They are far ahead now.

Except for one big male. He lags at the rear, foraging at leisure.

I rush him.

He turns to me and lowers his head, with two corkscrew horns. He charges.

I turn away in amazed terror, but too late. A horn catches my left rear thigh. It rips into me with seering pain. I yank my thigh free. The goat comes at me again. I growl, a shrieking scream of a growl.

The goat stops, stamps, snorts. Then leaves.

The hole in my thigh is deep and wide, but the wound may not be as grave as it is painful, for as I lick, the blood stops flowing.

This is a lesson, O great hunter Orasmyn: Never attack dangerous beasts unless they are weak.

Another lesson: Don't assume they are weak.

I loll onto my back and would sleep, when I remember the leopard. And tigers. The night holds predators, predators who see better in the dark than lions.

But maybe even lions hunt at night. After all, I look for food whenever I can, night or day, regardless of the limitations of my sight. Maybe this behavior conforms to lion behavior.

And maybe this night holds lions who would hunt me now — for with my wound, I might be prey, rather than friend, to them.

I get to my feet with difficulty and limp to the nearest group of boulders. They are arranged poorly, however, with no natural hole or cave. But I cannot search further. This much activity has already made my wound bleed again. I dig into the earth under a boulder — but, though I am an excellent digger, the earth is exceedingly hard. When I'm out of energy, I settle in. I lick my wound until I fall asleep.

The morning sun heats the rock above me. I pant in my shallow hole. It has taken weeks to get this far. Full summer heat shimmers over the land. My thirst hurts. But I stay in this hole and sleep as much as I can.

Another night passes. Another day.

By the third afternoon I cannot bear my thirst. I creep from my hole and stretch. My wound heals well. I hardly limp as I walk, but I know enough not to try trotting.

Beast

The thickness and closeness of the trees to the north signal water. I walk until I find the stream, which has formed a small pool. The water is blessedly sweet. The lushness of India seeps down my throat, through my belly, into my limbs and tail. Despite my hunger, I am home.

Something flashes white in the trees. I hurry away. When nothing follows, I come forward slowly, eyes scanning the branches. And there they are, high up. A small party of monkeys. Fifteen, at least. They have enormous ruffs of gray hair around black faces. But, oh, maybe that isn't their real color at all — that is only the impoverished information that these eyes give. Maybe they are tawny, as I know I must be, for they look strangely lionlike. Even their tails end in a bushy tuft. Their fur is long and sleek. They are staring at me. Almost all of them at once. Wary. Wide-cheeked.

I sit on my haunches and look back at them. What wonders this great land holds.

At length the monkeys get bored with me; they play with one another. And now they put their hands to their mouths and spit out something that they munch on. They spit and eat and spit and eat until their cheeks are narrow. Ha! They stored food in their cheeks like pouches.

Food.

I take a whiff. Fruits. The smell is not attractive to my lion nose, but I must stay alive. I can eat fruits.

A small way back from the pool stands a clumping of bushes. Perhaps berry bushes. I walk there slowly, careful not to strain my thigh. Berry bushes, all right, but they've been completely stripped of fruit.

My head drops in disappointment.

A high, squeaky trill comes from nearby rocks. I creep slowly. A white-footed mouse sings as though to the moon that is just becoming visible in the darkening sky. I pounce. The mouse races off, safe. But the earth sinks under my feet. A burrow, an underground nest.

I dig up the mouselings and eat their bald bodies in one gulp. I test the ground. More tunnels and burrows. In all, I find six nests. Enough only to whet my appetite.

But now I have the energy to go searching. I trot slowly, aware of my wound, but urged on by necessity. I make no sound.

Little growls ahead. The smell of meat. I trot faster; my paws make a soft scrunch on the earth.

Two lion cubs gnaw on a large piece of meat. I come closer. They see me and run. I fall on the meat, the whole leg of a large deer, and eat greedily.

The cubs watch from a safe distance. But one is bolder. He crouches and creeps forward on large feet.

I snarl, and he races back to his twin. But soon he creeps toward me again, his face hungry. The dark spots on his forehead give him a look of worried intensity. His mother will bring him food. No one will feed me. I snarl again. But the cub doesn't scare as easily now. He persists in coming forward. I growl. He settles himself on the other end of the leg and chews.

Now his timid twin joins him.

I give one last snarl, but make no move to chase them away. After all, what would I do if the bold one confronted me?

We eat with gusto, emitting little rolling growls and hums of pleasure.

Growl!

I get to my feet as fast as my wound allows. The cubs meow and whine.

The lioness approaches slowly, her head low, ears back, eyes wide open. She growls louder.

I am loath to leave while meat still clings to the bone of the deer, yet that growl is daunting. I run a fair distance, then stop and watch. A thin line of blood streams hot down my thigh again.

The cubs bang around their mother's legs now. They lick her face. Then they go back to the meat. The lioness looks long at me and growls. She turns and goes back a ways, picks up something in her mouth, and carries it to the cubs. Another leg. She drops it, flops down with a loud sigh, and eats.

Roar!

I run as fast as I can, crashing through the underbrush, back up into the mountains from where I came. I find a wide ledge and collapse. Gradually, calmness returns.

That was the first true roar I've heard other than the ones I've produced myself. But I didn't stay long enough to see the lion who made it. My heart quickens again at the memory.

At last I sleep.

When I wake, it is night. Something's wrong. I check this body, which is now familiar. My wound doesn't bleed; my belly is almost full. Yet something is definitely wrong. There is a noise in the back of my head. A rhythmic noise I cannot quite recognize.

I sleep again.

I wake to the midday sun. My belly lies heavy on the warm rock. From this vantage point I can see a long way. But I don't care to. And that noise is louder—each beat is like a word. Yes, I can discern it now: *taj*—crown—a single word chanting over and over inside this wide head of mine. I close my eyes and drift in and out of sleep.

For days I stay that way. Three days. Six. I lose count. I am thirsty. My belly is empty. But nothing stirs me from this rock.

The cubs allowed me to eat because they thought they had no choice.

The lioness allowed me nothing.

The chant in my head mocks me. *Taj.* The image of

Father in his royal garb fills my head so that I can see nothing else. I will never wear a crown, either in Persia or here in India. All that travel to get here was pointless.

I might as well lie on this rock until the sun dries me to a hairy hide.

I sleep. Day and night.

My sight blurs. My ears dull. My tongue swells.

I sleep.

Or am I dead?

The question isn't even interesting.

The sun blankets me. Cooks me. Prepares me as a sacrifice.

This all began with the Feast of Sacrifices. With the offering to the Merciful One. I have been transformed, from the one who offers to the offering itself. But to whom am I being sacrificed? To the *pari*? The remnant of spirit that remains in me rebels. I would rather be food to a tiger than strengthen the powers of that *pari*.

The chant in my head changes:

> There is only one God, and that is God.
>   And all else but God is nothing.
> There is only one God, and that is God.
>   And all else but God is nothing.
> There is only one God, and that is God.
>   And all else but God is nothing.

It goes on and on and on and on. The words lose their meaning, but they keep going. They carry me beyond their sense. They carry me someplace new. Someplace euphoric.

I rise on unsteady feet in a state of intoxication. The steepness of the mountain and the emptiness of my body should pitch me over the rocks to my death. But this thought brings no fear. I know my feet will prevail. I descend without mishap, half floating, half dancing.

I go to the pool in the stream and drink. The chant in my head has been replaced with my senses. I see and smell and hear everything. For a moment I believe I glimpse *tawhid*—the unity that bridges the distance between human and God.

A little way back from the edge of the water I find a pile of rotting figs. Whoever gathered these must have been interrupted. They are not fit for consumption by anything but garbage eaters now. I swallow one, willing myself not to taste or smell, mastering these senses. My stomach writhes at the nasty intrusion. But the fig stays down. I swallow another. And another. Slowly I eat the entire pile.

It takes only a day of drinking and digesting to clear my mind. I am Orasmyn. I need no one's help. I can do this.

CHAPTER TEN

My Pride

Over the next few months I trail the lion family, whose members meet at random intervals, then disperse over their territory. There's one large male with tufts at his elbows, three females, a young male of perhaps a year with a light muzzle, and the two cubs, who are weaned and spend most of their day playing. It's a small pride, I have learned through investigation. Neighboring prides live to the east and south, across the swirling river that must be the Indus. I've found them by their roars, observing from a hiding place. The east pride has seven lionesses and numerous cubs. The south pride is even larger. Each pride avoids the others, roaring loudly whenever they happen to come within sight of one another.

The largest pride has three adult males; the middle

pride, two; and the pride I follow has only one. Perhaps the number of males tolerated depends on the number of females. Whatever the case, I am quite sure I cannot be adopted by the small pride. That first roar I heard from the unseen lion gave me that message. Still, I can learn from the small pride. That's my goal. And nothing can stop me from thinking of them as my pride.

I learn to scratch my ears with my hind paws. I practice strutting, like a male before a female. I rake my claws downward on tree trunks to sharpen them. I roar in the early morning. I flick my ears to get rid of invading flies. I retreat to the shade of a dried-out sunken riverbed at noon. I even sniff at the branches where males have urinated, and I train myself to spray urine and anal gland secretions around the perimeter of the small outcropping of rocks where I prefer to sleep. No one else would want this place; still, my strong odor marks it as my territory just in case.

But none of it means anything, for I continue to blunder as a hunter. I race at my prey too soon. Or they hear me coming when I'm still far away.

When the lionesses bring down a kill, I watch from a safe distance until they've left. Then I hurry to the carcass before the other carrion eaters can get there.

My pride's territory is rich with game; I thank the Merciful One for this every day. They need never cross the Indus River into the other prides' territories. That first meal I had with the cubs turned out not to be deer, though there are many deer in these woods, particularly a tiny, swift kind that barks when it's frightened. No, that meal was antelope, the largest kind I've ever seen. I easily recognize the carcass of most kinds of animals that live here now—no matter how little remains. To the south, where many bamboo grow, herds of wild oxen feed on the tender shoots. And there is even a kind of wild ass, quite light in color, and small. They run in pairs or in groups of five or six. I watched a lioness bring down a colt, but there was nothing left after the pride had finished feeding—nothing for me.

The trees teem with monkeys—not just the lion-like ones I saw on first arriving here, but also ones with funny short tails that curl upward in a single loop. These monkeys, too, carry food in pouches inside their cheeks. I almost caught a youngster once, and in his surprise, he spit a wad of lizard and seeds and insects, which I promptly ate. And then there are the monkeys that like to swim. They're noisy and quarrelsome, and the young ones continually chase each other. I gave up on trying to catch them long ago. But I never stop watching them. They can scream at each other over a favorite resting spot on a limb or a piece of fruit or anything, then the next moment they sit calmly side by side and groom each other's fur lovingly.

The members of my pride groom each other, too, especially the lionesses.

I close my eyes and remember Father hugging me, Mother holding my hands within hers. The memory seems a fantasy.

One day the lead lioness of my pride goes after a huge ox. I watch from a perch in a distant tree. Normally my pride feeds on calves, for the adult oxen have gigantic horns. This one is no exception. I tense at the danger, but also at the anticipation of a feast. The past week's food has been meager for me. Hunger is strong.

The lioness creeps close, slowly, ever so slowly. Then she springs into a run. The ox bolts, and the lioness drives him toward another lioness, lying in ambush, who rushes at him. I've seen this kind of maneuver before, of course. But the ox doesn't behave like a deer or antelope; he doesn't back up. He thunders straight on, head lowered, right for the second lioness.

A third lioness rises from the grass immediately beside the ox. She is the one who gave birth almost two months ago. Her belly skin has flapped since then, weighted down with her swollen mammaries. She shouldn't be here now—she shouldn't be in this danger. The ox would have trampled her if the lead lioness had driven him only slightly more to the left. He will kill her now. I leap from the tree. But before I can advance much, she springs onto his neck from the side. The ox flings his thick head with tremendous force, sending the lioness flying. But the first lioness is already attached to his rump, riding there, above the kicking hooves. And the second lioness has him by the throat. The third lioness jumps into the fray again.

The end is swift.

I retreat and climb the tree again to watch, overcome with admiration for their courage and intelligence. They communicated strategy to each other; they must have. That cooperation couldn't simply have been a product of the moment.

If only I could learn to communicate with them. If only I could be accepted into the pride.

They tear the limbs free and drag away as much of the carcass as they can.

I drop from my tree and run quickly to the remains, only to find a very old male lion also running to it. He is alone, clearly a nomad. He opens his black black muzzle to show fangs that are worn down to stumps. He roars at me.

I see this grandfather's ribs, and somewhere inside me the urge to be charitable stirs. *Zakat*. Yes, that is one of the pillars of my faith: Give to the poor. Oh, yes, Orasmyn still lives within me. Hungry though I am, I back up in gratitude to the Merciful One, who allows me this opportunity.

Soft yips come from bushes to the side. I recognize them instantly: jackals. They are grouping.

I look at the old lion. We both know that if I leave this meat to him, the jackals will take it from him, anyway. He is doomed.

I roar.

The old one wanders off.

I eat my fill. As I leave, the jackals descend.

For two days I rest, satiated. On the third morning I rise for a leisurely walk. I spot three young bachelor lions traveling together across my pride's territory. I follow at a distance.

Roar.

That is the sound of my pride's male, as distinctive as his face. He must have heard these bachelors or smelled them or seen them, though he isn't anywhere in sight.

The largest of the three young males runs toward the roar. The two others trot along slowly, as do I — but I am always in hiding. Still, I stay as close as I dare. I must not miss a single second of what is about to happen. My hopes are a jumble I cannot untangle.

My pride's male stands in view now, large and

commanding. He charges the intruders. The young male turns fast and runs away. His companions run even faster. I stay hidden.

The ruling male allows the intruders to escape. He turns and walks off.

He still has his pride. The bachelors still have nothing. These are the customs: If I want my own pride, I must fight the ruling male for it. And I could never win against the male of my pride. I am alone.

Like the tiger.

I've seen only one tiger so far, and only three times at that. But he's always alone. He seems to prefer night hunting. And he swims in the huge river almost as though he likes it. Then he disappears into the jungle on the east side of the river. I'm grateful he never crosses to this side.

That side of the river is home to another kind of loner, too: the rhinoceros. I've watched them browse on twigs and grass, completely calm, even when the tiger passes.

But I am neither tiger nor rhinoceros. I am not meant to live alone.

I return to my rock ledge and sleep.

That night I wander for hours. The next morning, when I'm dozing in the sun, a lioness from my pride comes out of a thicket carrying a cub by its shoulders. Three other cubs follow on her heels. They don't see me, but I'm delighted to see them. She's kept the cubs well-hidden these two months. Once I was sure I knew where they were, but when I got up the nerve to investigate, she had moved them. Only the matted grasses and milky musk told that they'd been there. I'm convinced she moved them every few days. But it's clear they can now move easily by themselves. The one hanging from her mouth thrashes after a while. She drops it, and it joins the others, running in crazy zigzags around her legs.

The lioness patiently leads her cubs to a new thicket. She licks them all over, then leaves.

Without hesitation, I go to the thicket. The small cubs rest on top of one another, in a pile. They come to attention and look at me with huge eyes. They hiss. I lie down with my jaw resting on the ground between my forepaws. The cubs jump and yowl around me, trying to scare me off. I stare at them calmly. Finally, one comes close and sniffs at my paw. I blink. The cub comes to my face. I lift my head as slowly as I can. The cub freezes. I lick his leg. He smells my face. Then he offers me his side. And I lick this small creature from shoulder to rump. The other three come along for their baths, despite the fact that their mother has just licked them. Greedy for attention. I roll them over with my muzzle. I rub my forehead on their fat milk bellies. Two males, two females. The males' jaws are wider, but all have the most wonderfully expressive faces. One of the females grunts. I don't know what it means, but I get up quickly and leave.

That very night the weather changes. Rain comes in. It pours for days. But nothing stops me from watching the cubs. The lioness moved them after my first visit. Undoubtedly she picked up my scent. But I followed her to the little cave, where they've been ever since.

The cubs peek out into the rain now, one after another, and finally give in to their exuberance and romp outside, rolling on top of each other through the mud. I join in.

I visit them every day, some days twice, some days three times. They meow and leap on me in greeting. They lick my face. They attack my tail, and I flick it at them as though it's the fiercest snake. They are my joy.

Today I take a new route to the cave. A noisy buzz catches my attention. Bees swarm around a hollow tree. Their nest has been raided. Despite the rain, it's easy to follow the scent of honey to a hole in the ground. I dig furiously. The honey badger wakes and scrambles to get away. I bite into its back. The animal turns inside its loose skin and sinks its teeth into my nose. It scratches my cheeks with its enormous claws. I ignore the pain and open my jaws just enough to get a bigger bite, then I clamp down with all my might.

The badger goes limp instantly. I eat every part I can — my first wild kill other than mouselings — every part but the liver, the choicest morsel. I look around for any honeycomb that might remain. After all, it seems like a lifetime since I had a dessert, and honey is the best dessert. But the badger must have eaten all of it.

So I go tardy to my cubs, but with a gift: I drop the liver on the ground, and they fight over it, more out of curiosity than anything else, for their mother still nurses them. And now they've discovered the evidence of my struggle with the honey badger. They lick the bite marks on my nose, the scratches on my cheeks. The bolder female, my favorite one, rakes her claws through my mane, getting out the dirt that's entangled where I cannot reach.

Grooming me; this youngster is grooming me.

A reedlike spirit within me cries. I stretch as long as I can, so as much of me as possible can receive their tender gift.

The cubs crawl all over me, tumbling happily, unaware of the tumultuous feelings in my chest. My little female hums, like the lioness back at the hunting park in Tabriz. And the amazing thought comes: In a few months they will eat meat. Then I can steal my favorite female. She can live with me, and I'll bring her the leftovers from her pride. And when she's adult, she'll hunt for both of us, for I have seen how the male waits while the females hunt. It will come naturally to her. We will rub heads and groom each other and raise cubs and grow old together.

India holds the answer, after all.

I will overcome the worst of the *pari*'s curse: I will not pass the rest of my life alone. I am Prince Orasmyn. I need nothing from my old life, I need no one.

Roar!

The mother lioness lunges at me.

I jump away.

We circle each other in front of the mouth of the cave. Already I hear the other lionesses running. Within moments my back is to the cave, and I'm surrounded on all other sides. The cubs whine and whimper in confusion. The adults growl and roar savagely, in synchrony. They snap at me. I whip myself around, roaring back as ferociously as I know how. One well-landed slash of their claws would cripple me for good. I am lion meat.

A cub runs between my legs. I trip and roll toward a lioness at one side. Astonishingly, she backs up with a growl. I get to my feet and run straight past her. The ruling male appears from nowhere — he runs after me. But he's not even trying to catch me. He chases at a slow pace. Just to let me know I don't belong, I'm not welcome. This is not my home.

I am lion, and I am not lion.

And I am alone.

The lionesses in Father's hunting park accepted me because there were no other males around. But in the wilds of India, no lioness will accept me. And even if one happened to, even if I stole that little female and made her mine, a bachelor lion would come along and take her away before long.

I am doomed to loneliness. And to living off the refuse of others.

The ruling male gives one final roar.

I feel the sound in my bones long after it dies from the air.

CHAPTER ELEVEN

Traveling Again

The cobra rears.

I am cornered under the low rock ledge where I slept last night.

The cobra's neck flattens into a hood almost as wide as my head. Its body bunches in zigzags under it, but I can tell it is long. Maybe twice as long as my body. A king cobra.

One bite would kill a man.

The urge to run tightens me like rock. I fight it. There is not enough room for me to pass safely. My jaw aches to roar, a wasted act on the deaf snake.

The snake head moves slightly, as though floating on a breeze I cannot feel. Its eyes hold me. It flickers a split tongue.

I don't know what to do. But I can't bear this waiting. I bolt.

And I'm free. Alive and well past the striking range of those fangs. I stop and look back.

The snake glides slowly into my spot. It coils up and lies still.

I have no idea why I am still alive. But I recognize the cobra's gesture as a farewell from India, appropriate, since I had already decided to leave. The territory of the small pride is two days' walk behind me.

I travel west, into Persia. My country offers no welcome; I don't harbor delusions. I go to Persia on a mission—to get the treasure waiting for me in the hunting park of Tabriz. What will come after that is beyond my ability to reason. My thoughts come to a halt. I know nothing except desire: I want that book from Mother.

I trot for days. Weeks. I don't know how long. Now and then I recognize a village from when I passed this way going to India. It seems I follow close to the same path in reverse, though not by design.

I raid the pet population for food again. And sometimes I indulge myself and creep close to a dwelling even when I'm not hungry, close enough to hear the people call to one another in early evening. They share the *tanour*—the flatbread I love—as they tell of the day just past and plan out the day to come. Because the Shah's family moved from palace to palace, I am familiar with many varieties of my native tongue. I used to find some of them coarse. Now they are all pure and fine, like the desert sands. I listen as long as I dare.

I am not crying. Listening to human language doesn't even hurt. I feel nothing.

India couldn't host me. Maybe no place can. Maybe I will spend the rest of my existence alone.

When the snow falls, my heart quickens. I steer clear of settlements now, for my tracks in this white fluff would lead to a wide-scale hunt, I'm sure. Excitement grows as I near Tabriz. Mother and Father won't be there, of course. The Tabriz palace stands empty in winter. But that's best, for seeing either of them would shatter this blessèd numbness that shields me from pain.

I enter through the eastern wall of the hunting park, reveling just briefly, just for a tiny moment, in the fantasy of returning home. A surprised buck gives a delicious meal, the first truly satisfying one in so long, and ridiculously easy to catch. When I finish, I move heavily. Particular trees are familiar now.

The slab of rock is exactly where I remembered it. The book lies there innocently, as though it's trivial, frozen into the dirt under the rock. My *Gulistan.* Though I haven't even read it, in this moment it is all that I cherish. I dig the book free, careful not to damage it, and burrow my way under the bottom, snow-laden branches of a pine. I set the book on the ground and sink beside it, ready to sleep with my head resting on its cover.

Rattle.

I cannot see in the pitch-dark under this snow house, but I know that sound: a crested porcupine. The rattle is close and grows louder. I jump to my feet and crash out through the branches.

But the book still lies in the porcupine's lair. Precious book. Stupid me.

There's no chance of sneaking in without the porcupine knowing. Stupid, stupid me.

I growl. When the porcupine doesn't emerge, I plunge back through the branches.

Pain pierces my right front paw, explodes up through my leg. I scream as I search. Here it is, my book, my *Gulistan.* I take it in my jaws and tumble quickly out again. More pain in my rear. Bursts of heat.

I limp to another pine nearby and burrow under, this time advancing tentatively, smelling for the fruity odor of porcupine. Nothing but the scent of dried needles.

I bite porcupine quills from my flanks and from my paw. Four altogether. I must have practically stepped on the cursèd creature. My wounds flame. I moan myself to sleep.

Beast

My flank heals quickly, but my paw swells and oozes pus. I lick it roughly between feverish naps. For a long time I stay in the shelter of the pine, going out only to stretch and eat snow. I'm lucky that the buck was so large; several days pass before hunger gnaws at me again. By this time, though, my paw is on the mend.

I leave the pine boughs and walk west, the book in my mouth. Soon I'm at the palace. I wander through my private *belaq*, then out into the public gardens, and, finally, to the rose garden. The snow is not deep, and I can easily see that these bushes have been tended carefully—pruned and mulched in preparation for winter exactly as I would have ordered. Kiyumars has been faithful.

Life has gone on here without me. And it will keep going on without me.

As though I'm dead. The man is dead.

The lion lives. And nothing makes sense.

The sun sets, the night blows frigid, the moon cuts the star-filled sky, the sun rises again, and still, I sit in this rose garden with the book in my jaws, stiff in every joint. Do I await inspiration? Has Orasmyn become such a fool that he simply waits for answers to come? Even the patience of the Merciful One must be taxed.

I lay the book on the ground and do my *rakatha*. I

pray inside my head. When I finish, I listen to my thoughts. All they can whisper is, *Gulhaye sourkh* — roses.

Am I losing my mind?

But the whisper continues, light and sweet, with the charm of a woman's words to a small child. They are like salve.

I remember the French man who walked here with my father years ago and boasted that French roses were the best in the world. And the book I hold in my mouth is named *Gulistan — Rose Garden.*

Prickles of hope go up my neck, hum in my ears, tingle in my mouth.

I open the book. Even in this cold it falls open easily, thawed by the heat of my mouth. I read eagerly. But my eyes have trouble finding the words, staying on the page. I force them. This is nourishment for my soul at last. Work for me, my eyes. Please, please work for me.

I read of a *qadi,* an Islamic judge, drinking wine with a lover, murmuring words of desire about the sun and the moon and the pearls of the ocean. They pass the night in lovemaking, only to be discovered by the king in the morning. But the *qadi* wins the king's pardon through a witty defense.

The words run together again. I want to know more, but I cannot read. These eyes will not work right. I slap the book shut with my paw, throw my head back in frustration, and open my jaw. I stop myself from roaring only at the very last moment. My roar would terrify all of Tabriz.

I close my eyes and wait. When they feel rested at last, I open them and force them to read again. The book has fallen open at a new place. The poem before me sings of a soul in a beautiful man's body, now in a woman's body, now a mouse, now a tiger. Always dancing, knowing love everywhere, moving through the infinite, through the breath and laughter of the Merciful One. Saadi's verses whirl with passion; they take flight in a divine madness. They say love is the water of life.

I turn my head to the left and say those words again, so they will be impressed upon my heart: Love is the water of life.

And I am laughing myself, in my crazy leonine way. Laughing. For I know now. The *pari* said only the love of a woman could undo the curse. Oh, yes, it's true. For through the love of a woman, I can know the love of the Merciful One. Passion leads to compassion.

Thank you, Mother. Thank you. Thank you, Saadi. Thank you, Merciful One.

What a mistake it was to go to India. I know now my true course. The French grow roses. And Frenchwomen give the perfume of roses—that's what the Frenchman said to Father years ago. So they must love roses the most. The woman I will love, the woman who will love me, lives in France. Somehow I must find her.

That whisper in my head, that whisper of roses, was the seed of a plan I cannot yet comprehend, but in which I place all my trust.

I take the book in my jaws and head north.

CHAPTER TWELVE

Two Years

I trot night and day, up into the Alborz Mountains,
then west, on and on into the Caucasus range. Winter winds blow bitter here. Holding the book in my
mouth becomes a torment; icicles form from my drool.
I trot more slowly, week in, week out. I stop only to
raid the animals of the tiny settlements that litter
these mountains. I sleep only when I drop from
exhaustion. Still, I cover so little ground.

The northern coast of the Black Sea finally guides
my path truly to the west. While the coast offers easy
terrain, my frustration mounts every time I come to a
cove that I know I could swim across more swiftly
than run around. But I cannot figure out how to swim
and still keep my *Gulistan* dry. The Sea of Azov,
which connects to the Black Sea, practically breaks
my spirit; swimming the strait would have saved me

weeks of travel. But, then, the cold of the sea might have killed me. So perhaps this book saves my body, as well as my soul.

Spring comes, with drenching rains. I form lairs for myself under the lowest branches of towering spruce. The rain wouldn't harm me, of course, but it would destroy my heart's last remaining treasure. I lose so much time waiting for the rains to stop. My impatience prickles the skin under my thick winter coat, which sheds in clumps.

Sunny days return with greater frequency, and I trot again, once more through mountains, now the Carpathians. Mountain travel is slower than travel on level ground, but safer because of the infrequency of other travelers and the abundance of caves to hide in. And now that it is summer, the mountains are not as hot as I imagine the valleys to be. These are strong advantages.

Still, by the time I reach the end of this mountain range, autumn has given way to winter again. The advantages of mountain travel must be foregone in the interest of speed. I head not southwest for the Alps, as I had originally planned, but, instead, directly west across the rolling lands into the lush forests of Germany. France is not far now. My legs trot with renewed energy.

I follow roads, ears alert. At the slightest noise that

hints of humans, I race into the woods. Sometimes my fear clutches so strong that I keep running for days. Such behavior thwarts me, for when I panic like that, I lose my sense of direction and set myself back in this endless journey. But I am unable to suppress these episodes of terror, and with reason. What remains of human knowledge in me recognizes the brutal truth: Every town presents mortal threat. Indeed, every stranger happened upon in a bend in the road is a potential enemy. All of them carry pistols.

At night I see men on the roads get robbed, sometimes by marauding soldiers. I grow thin and anxious. After I see a man shot for his purse, I hide in the woods. My pacing wears a smooth, deep path in front of the hole I have dug to sleep in. This journey is surely ill-fated. I cannot face the road again. I pace.

But the promise of roses finally lures me. I erase the image and sound of pistols from my brain. All that matters is motion. I go onward into this wet cold that enters my bones, and onward through a spring of noisy farmers, a summer of adventure-seeking wanderers, an autumn that opens with dangerously frequent markets.

Trotting forever, my *Gulistan* between my jaws.

The leaves are dry and falling again by the time I reach France, by the time I finally, finally rest.

PART 4

New World

CHAPTER THIRTEEN

A Man

I've been sleeping among my roses. A small garden yet, but one I treasure; each rosebush cost me dearly. I prowled the countryside for flower gardens, all of which have roses. I dug up the smallest bush in each garden, the one that was least likely to be missed, and carried it home gently between my teeth to replant here. All at night.

This is my garden. My pleasure.

The Frenchman who talked with Father was right: France has the best roses in the world. Indeed, it seems this part of the world grew from my heart, for roses and jasmine are undoubtedly the most popular flowers. Their sweetness saturates the night air.

Night comforts me, offers me protection. Few humans walk the roads at night hereabouts, and those who do are often intoxicated — and easily dodged. And

no humans wander off the roads into the countryside at night.

During the day I stay at home.

Home is an abandoned castle yet a luxurious
one—it even has glass window panes. My knowledge
of its history came piecemeal and remains frag-
mented. Early one evening, only days after I had
moved in, a pair of young lovers came sneaking
through the brambles and overgrown wisteria that
form a natural barrier around the castle grounds.
They entered through the front door.

I watched from the upstairs hall that overlooks
both the entranceway and the interior grand staircase. She was bareheaded—face and hair, as is the
crude habit of the women here. He was clean-shaven
and wore no hat—a peasant youth. They undressed
and lay in each other's arms, offering my eyes the inti-
mate curve of their bodies, the generous heat of their
affection.

A moan escaped my lips.

They grabbed their clothes and ran.

I didn't know if they had seen me. But I needed to
know. For if they had, I would have had to abandon
this most perfect dwelling.

The young couple ran to the road, where she
mounted a horse and left. He raced off across the
meadow on foot.

I followed him, rather than her, for the horse she rode got skittish at the whiff of me, and I knew he'd give me away. But the meadow foiled me—there was no cover in the evening light. So I had to stick to the woods at the meadow's edge, taking the long way around at the fastest lope I could manage.

The man finally cut through a stand of evergreens and came out at a house on the edge of a farm. Two other youths sat behind the house, drinking from jugs and talking loudly. My man ran up to them, grabbed a jug, and took a swig. Then he spoke, and, though his words were in a variety of French that differed much from the Parisian I once studied, I could understand at least the gist of it; he told of going to the castle—of my moan.

I stayed in a crouch, hidden by shadows in the undergrowth, while they talked of the ghost that inhabits my castle. A few years back the castle was abandoned in great haste after a terrible tragedy. The ghost reigns still. It took several minutes for me to realize they attributed my moan to that ghost.

Since then, all winter long and into the start of this spring, no one has come through the brambles.

Oh, a boy child came nosing around a couple of weeks ago. But I gave a small growl from behind a tree, and he screamed, *"Fantôme!"* and ran so fast, he slipped and tumbled.

I haven't seen evidence of the infamous ghost on the castle grounds, but I am ready enough to play ghost. And I am grateful that the mysterious world of spirits benefits me in at least this way, after all the harm the *pari* has done me.

No one must come until I am ready.

The rest of my knowledge of this castle stems from the library, within which is volume after volume in French, as well as Latin and Greek and Chinese, but also rolled maps of the world and of France and of this locality. The castle is in the southwest of France, not more than a day's journey from the sea. I have no desire to travel to the sea or anywhere else. My travels have ended. This castle is my refuge.

And a well-stocked refuge, thanks to the fear of the ghost that keeps would-be thieves at bay.

I am in control of my life here. I need no one's help.

I look beyond my rose garden to what was once a flamboyant arrangement of flower gardens circling cherry laurels and silvery olive trees. All is edged by cypress that stay fresh year-round, so thick that the castle is invisible from the road below. Much of the gardens revived with my care. The roses didn't come back, though. That's why I had to gather them from others' gardens.

Autumn is a tricky time to transplant rosebushes. I pruned away only injured branches. Then I dug generous holes and spread the roots carefully within. I covered each plant halfway up the main stem with a mulch of twigs. With the help of the lucky rain that comes almost daily, they strengthened. A month ago I cleaned away the mulch for the start of spring.

The rosebushes bask in the morning sun on the southeast side of the castle. By afternoon, they are in shade. This is what I want, for roses that stand in filtered shade have a longer flowering season and give blooms of richer hues. I cannot see the hues, of course, but their beauty is an important part of my plan.

The drive from the road to the main entrance is on the north side. It is completely blocked by the brambles I've encouraged to spread. To the left stands a dovecote with an exterior rotating ladder and nesting places for eighteen hundred birds. I counted them, as I clung to the ladder and cleaned the perches. When I first came, there were only a couple of hundred birds. Now the nests are all full. Sometimes in the morning when they're warbling loudest, I close my eyes and feel I'm back in Tabriz, in the men's pavilion, not far from the pigeon tower.

A massive gate leads into the courtyard, which is protected by a wall and reinforced by a moat. The moat had gone dry; leaves and sticks and the debris of storms had clogged the large aquaducts from the stream beyond the woods. It was easy to clear out and adapt for my *wudhu*. At first I thought I might swim in it, too. But this body I inhabit takes no joy in swimming.

I stand now and stretch, letting my nose press forward into a cluster of rosebuds that already perfume the air in the most delicate of ways. Hunger excites me. I haven't eaten for four days—not because of lack of food. The countryside around here has abundant hares and hedgehogs and foxes—all easy prey given the hunting skills I've gradually acquired. But I prefer to take down larger animals, eat until I can hardly move, and then sit digesting for days, getting up only for a drink or to wander a bit or to pray. Usually by the third or fourth day, I feel energetic enough to work on preparing the castle and expanding the gardens—a task I perform assiduously.

All as part of my plan. I began gathering rosebushes to make this garden for my own solace. But as I read more and more of Saadi's verses, I realized that this garden holds an even greater hope. I must make the garden inviting, enticing. Then I will lure a woman here. And she will walk through the rose garden on her own. She will run. She will dance. She will love my *gulistan*. And then she will come to love the other gardens. And the dovecote. And the castle. She will love the whole magical world within the perimeter of brambles.

And she will love the creator of this magic.

I will win the love of a woman and undo the *pari*'s curse.

And once I am human again, I will take my bride and return to the company of humans, to the community that is my birthright.

It is time now to tend to my gardens. I nose through the daylily shoots on the north border of the property. There are hundreds. I leave dozens undisturbed, so they can keep multiplying, but the rest I dig up and pile at the edge of the rose garden. I scratch the dirt close to the base of each rosebush, just enough to set in the daylily roots so that their tops will be barely covered. Daylilies form an ideal ground cover for a rose garden. They reduce both the need to water and the diseases that afflict roses so easily.

The job consumes the entire day. By the time I've finished, my hunger is fierce.

Tonight will be good hunting.

But first things first.

I go to the moat and perform the *wudhu*. Then I walk inside the castle to the library.

I face the southeast window, toward Mecca, and lower my nose to the floor, keeping my legs rigid. I do not crouch, for crouching is too easy in feline form. Hanging forward like this is difficult; it helps me remember that I must be ready to sacrifice all for the Merciful One. I pray.

Finally, I'm ready for the treat. I walk slowly around the library.

A few days ago I finished reading a book by the Greek philosopher Aristotle. The book still lies on the chair, where I left it. I nudge it with my muzzle until it sticks out over the edge, then I take it between my teeth and walk to the shelves. I rise on my hind feet, tilt my head as far as it can go to one side, and try to slide the book back on the shelf. It drops to the floor.

For a brief moment I indulge in pointless anger. I am like the worst of criminals, deprived of both hands, despised by the masses. Indeed, my punishment is even more cruel, for I am completely isolated from both the masses and family. I lift my head and roar.

Then I calm myself.

I wedge the book between my paws and press until the bound edge pushes upward. I take it again between my paws and try to replace it on the shelf. After the fourth attempt, the book stays.

It's time to select another book, for these books give my only opportunity to keep language strong inside me, language, which is the human vehicle for prayer—my lifeline. While I regularly reread *Gulistan*, I alternate my other reading between books for pleasure and books for research. The Aristotle book gave pure pleasure—mental gymnastics. Today I should begin a book of the other sort.

My eyes scan for a volume that might tell of sorcery, of fairy spells and how to break them. It isn't that I fool myself into thinking I will find a novel way to undo the *pari*'s curse. No. The fairies of the Europeans have little in common with the Persian ones. Rather, a book of that sort would make me feel less alone. For the very existence of such a book would mean that others have suffered like I do.

Perhaps others have formed plans of escape.

Perhaps they have succeeded.

I shudder as I pass the shelf of Chinese books. Rumi and Saadi, the great poets, survived Mongol invasions, but those invasions destroyed whole populations of Persian cities. For this reason Father never allowed Chinese books in our palaces.

I walk quickly back to the shelf that holds the Aristotle book and read each title nearby.

Clouds darken the room a little. A storm comes. Though my gardens are already speckled with flower buds, winter hasn't completely given up yet. I must hurry, or I'll lose all chance to read today. My eyes alight on a leather cover embossed with beautiful lettering. *Aeneid*.

I open and read, concentrating hard so that my eyes can follow the print:

> *Arma virumque cano Troiae qui primus ab oris*
> *Italiam fato profugus Laviniaque venit . . .*

Beast

The poet sings of a man tossed about on land and sea by the anger of the goddess Juno, so that he leaves his home in Troy and goes to Italy, where he suffers much in war before finally founding a city.

I, too, have traveled far, always tormented by the harshest anger of the *pari*. The hero of this poem interests me. I read on, turning the pages carefully with the very tip of my tongue touching the smallest part of the corner of each page. I read of Aeneus' shipwreck and how the gods disagree and of this hero's going onshore in Africa. But when I get to the part where Aeneus slays a deer, hunger stops me.

The room has darkened considerably, anyway. My eyes become unruly.

The artistry of this epic falls short of the *Shahnameh*, certainly, and its passion in comparison to that of *Gulistan* is like a candle flicker to the sunlight. Nevertheless, it holds my attention. I leave the book on the floor, where I've been crouched reading it, and I take a dry quill from the desk and drop it on the open page to save my spot if a breeze should come. I lower my head and rest first one cheek on the page, then the other—giving thanks to the author and to the Merciful One for allowing me to read.

I pad outside to the brambles and move under them. I am as low to the ground as I can go—as low as the lioness who I watched hunt the stag in the hunting park of my own palace in Tabriz. Beyond the brambles in this direction lies a quiet forest.

Instantly my spirit transforms; away from the castle my needs and pleasures belong to the lion that I am. Alert. Powerful. I am at home in these woods. And it feels good.

Within moments musty fungus smells invade my nostrils. The earth is rooted up here. I follow a path of fresh holes. The wetness of the earth in this part of the world never ceases to amaze me. Dead wood has been overturned not long ago. Ants scurry to rebuild their disturbed nests. I follow the path more quickly, for I recognize the signs.

And there's the wild boar. He sees me, despite the storm clouds that gather to block the sun. He is easily twice the weight I was in man form, with tusks as long as my front paw. Without warning, he runs at me and he is swift.

I flee toward the castle. The hooves of the beast pound behind me. He gains on me. I leap onto a low tree limb, climb to a higher branch, crouch.

The boar runs stupidly past.

I stay unmoving for a long while.

He is gone. French boars are huge compared with Persian ones. Their tusks are absurdly long. The depth of his footprints should have told me that this one was too large for me to attack. I have accumulated knowledge over the past two and a half years and I have discovered that certain feral instincts take over at unexpected times. But now and then I ignore information that I should be using. This was such a time.

I killed a young boar last autumn—a very small boar. The Merciful One forbids the eating of pork, and as a man I never tasted it. But my lion eyes saw food. And in the *Shahnameh*, Bizhan hunts a boar—why, even the great Rustam roasts a wild boar. So the Merciful One forgives me, I am sure. That illustration of Rustam is one of my favorites, all gold and metallic green.

I miss colors.

The ground is far below, but I am calm. Trees don't present problems to me anymore. I don't prefer them as a place to rest, but I also don't hesitate to use them when the need arises, going for low, slanted branches if possible. I look around now. All I can see in the dimming light are more trees.

And a badger. It has come to eat the roots left behind by the boar. Funny little opportunist. Its long, grizzled fur is caked with mud. It's been wading in the pond nearby. My lungs swell as the short legs carry the stout body closer. I know my range well, so I wait, patient.

Rain falls softly, and the temperature plummets. If

it keeps up, the branch will grow slippery with ice and I'll lose my grip.

And, oh, an ice storm could damage my roses. The buds are close to blooming. I should return to the castle and cover them with the piles of crushed oak leaf that I brushed together when cleaning out the perennial garden.

But I'm hungry. And this badger cannot take forever to come within range.

Still, the badger does take its time. My patience wanes. Now it noses through a low bush, eating hard, dried-out bilberries. Closer. Closer.

I position myself in a crouch, ready.

The rain turns to sleet. The branch grows slick.

I leap.

Too soon. The beast turns and waddles furiously toward what I now see is the opening of his burrow.

I remember the bite of the honey badger back in India—the day the lion cubs groomed me, the day I was driven from my pride. I stop and watch the badger disappear into the burrow.

I could dig it out. But it isn't worth facing those teeth.

I lick my own nose as though I've been bitten.

The wind is high. I walk through the woods again, on the lookout for signs of the boar.

It snows now. A silly little roebuck huddles under

a bush, eyes closed against the wind, almost as though he's offering himself.

I kill the miniature deer with one bite to the throat. The snow comes thick, driven by the wind. I'm dragging the roebuck whole between my front legs back to the castle. I will stash him in the entranceway while I cover the rosebushes with mulch.

That's when I hear the whinny.

The man sits astride the skittish horse, trying to calm her. But the mare has caught my scent or the scent of the dead roebuck or both, and is half crazed by the storm, anyway. She tosses her head and rears, wild-eyed.

"*Un château!*"—a castle—the man shouts, as if to the horse.

I make my way under the brambles, drop the roebuck, and follow horse and rider, staying low, though the snow comes so hard, I don't believe this man would be able to see me even if I stood tall so long as I stayed close to bushes.

The man dismounts and, with difficulty, leads the panicked mare into the stable. He pulls a cloth from his pocket and winds it around the poor mare's head so that she cannot see. She stops moving instantly. He pats her withers and spreads a blanket over her back. Then he takes a halter from the saddlebag and slips it over her head, tethering her to a post. He pulls off the bridle and bit, gives her a parting pat on the side of her neck, then leaves, closing the stable door behind him. He knocks on the front door of my castle, though it stands open. In French he asks, "Is anyone there?" His accent is pure Parisian. He bangs with both fists now, calling loudly. Finally he enters.

A man walks in my home.

I run to a window and look in. He's out of sight, still calling from the entrance hall. Now he turns and rushes outside. Has he recognized some trace of me? I stay against the wall, crouched low.

He scurries through the woods, bending often, picking up bits of wood. He goes back to the castle, his arms piled high. He puts down the wood and pulls the door shut behind him.

From the window I watch him build a fire in the large hearth.

It's been years since I've sat by a fire.

Oh, the winter here hasn't been harsh. It snows often, but the sun comes out brilliantly day after day, and the air is never mean, like in the country I passed through to get here. Still, the damp cold can penetrate my fur and make me shiver. Especially at night.

A fire.

The man shakes the snow off his cloak and wide-brimmed hat. He spreads the cloak over a chair and perches the hat on a tall corner of the chairback. Next, he takes off his shoes and stockings, then his outer clothes. He stretches them on the floor in front of the fire. An oil lamp rests in a holder to the side of the fireplace. He lights the wick and carries the lamp ahead of him as he goes into the chapel. He doesn't pray, though. He merely looks around. And now he's going into the library. I watch him kneel on the floor and pick up the book I was reading. He places it carefully on the desk, not disturbing the open page. I like the respectful way he touches the books. O Merciful One, if only I could talk with this man. A discussion about anything, any little thing, man to man.

A small rumble starts in the back of my throat. This is my voice — not fit for conversation.

I realize I've raised my head way far high. If the man turns this way, he'll see me. I lower my shoulders until my eyes barely see over the window ledge. My mane still protrudes above it, but it is so covered with snow, I doubt it will draw his attention.

The man goes from room to room, calling. Then he climbs the stairs.

I sleep in the southeast room upstairs, so that I can look out over my rose garden before shutting my eyes and so that I can wake at the first hint of dawn and face Mecca. A blanket lies in a crumpled heap in the middle of the floor of my bedroom. That's what I sleep on. Will he see bits of my fur?

There are weapons in this house: knives, swords, guns.

And the man probably carries a pistol himself.

I run from window to window, anxious to see this man the moment he comes back downstairs.

Now his lamp flickers as he descends the staircase. His face is wary. He wanders into the larder. He comes out with a small booty and carries it to the table near the fireplace. He pulls up a chair. Then he goes back to the larder. He comes out with a bottle of wine and a bowl.

He lays dried fruits in the bowl, covers them with wine, then waits. While he waits, he drinks from the bottle. After a long time, he picks up the now plumped-up fruits and chews big.

Then he stands before the fire, slowly turning. He's drying out the underclothes he wears, toasting himself. Finally, he climbs the stairs again.

I listen, hoping to hear evidence that he sleeps. But, though the snow has stopped, the wind has gained momentum, and I hear nothing but the slapping of branches against one another. I go inside via the corner window that I broke the very first time I entered this castle, for I cannot pull the massive door open with my jaws. Once this man leaves, though, I'll be able to open the door from the inside, pushing outward. Then I'll let it stay slightly ajar as before, so that I can come and go as I please.

Once this man leaves. For he will leave. There's

nothing here to hold him. He came only because he got lost in the storm.

But he's here now. A man. In my home.

I don't want him to leave.

The bowl of fruit is still half full. The smell holds no attraction for me; meat is my only food. And the stench of the vinegary wine makes me sneeze. But the man can't hear me, just as I can't hear him. The fire lures me. I stretch out in its cradling warmth.

Then I remember the roebuck. It's buried in snow; it'll stay undisturbed until the morning.

I remember the rose garden. But by now the snow has already done its damage.

I sleep.

And dream of voices, human voices, his—with mine.

CHAPTER FOURTEEN

Gule Sourkh

Sunlight fills the room. A man descends the stairs. The man! The window I would leap from is on the far corner of the room—I'd have to cross the man's line of vision. How could I have let myself sleep so late? I run to the larder. But, no, that's the first place he'll go. I run to the chapel. Stupid me, of course he'll make morning prayers. I peek through the crack between the open chapel door and the wall. The man's kneeling by the fire, rebuilding it. I'm stuck in the chapel.

The man goes to the window and exclaims, "Spring!" He puts on the rest of his clothes and goes outside, leaving the door open.

I strain to see out through the door from where I hide in the chapel, and the sight baffles me. The snow has melted away entirely, and the sunshine is bright.

Yet the man's voice held no surprise, only happiness. This must be how spring behaves in this strange country.

The man is nowhere in sight.

I could bolt out the door, out the window—but he might be right around the corner, right in front of me. Besides, I don't really want to run away.

I want to know this man.

What an absurd thought. He would kill me.

But maybe not. He is a man who loves books. That much I saw in his behavior last night. Maybe he has a gentle soul.

I pace, crazy with indecision.

The man comes back in, leaving the door open behind him. He empties his pockets onto the table. A mound of old, dried acorns. Now he goes into the larder and comes out with a mortar and pestle and a goatskin bottle. He grinds the acorns and pours them into the bowl with the winey fruits from last night. He squeezes the goatskin. A glistening stream covers the mess in the bowl. The smell of rancid olive oil makes my nose wrinkle. The man eats every last morsel and scrapes the bottom of the bowl with his spoon.

He stands and comes to the chapel door.

I hide on the other side of the door, mouth closed to hold in my lion breath, my lion pants.

He enters and goes to the center of the small room.

He touches his forehead, chest, left shoulder, right shoulder—making the sign of the cross in the way I have seen Christians do. He kneels.

If he were to turn his head right now, he'd see me.

He bows his head and intones, *"Agnus Dei, qui tollis peccata mundi, miserere nobis. Gaudeamus in nomine Dei."*

I understand the Latin. The Lamb of God—I remember now, that's how Christians call Jesus. He has asked Jesus for pity, and asked further that he be allowed to rejoice in the name of the Merciful One. The man speaks of himself as "we," almost as though he's royal. But he travels alone in ordinary merchant's clothes, and he hasn't the manner of royalty. Perhaps this is the habit of Christians, to call themselves "we" before the Merciful One. Or perhaps he's praying not just for himself, but for everyone.

I like that possibility.

I like this man. If only we could talk to one another.

He stands.

He will turn now and discover me.

I can't think what to do. My body loses all feeling.

He backs out of the room.

I am half relieved, half disappointed.

The man goes outside now. I hurry into the main room and watch him from the window. He leads the mare up and down in front of the castle. She looks no worse for wear. Now they go around to the side.

"Mon Dieu!"—my God!

I look out the side window.

The man kneels over the roebuck I killed last night. He's inspecting its ragged throat. He looks every which way, jerking his head.

The mare nibbles on the grasses. The snow must have washed away my scent. She's calm.

But the man is now frantic. He grabs the mare's lead, puts on her bridle and bit, and takes off the halter. He mounts and circles the castle, looking for a road. Brambles meet him at every turn, until he comes back to the path the mare trampled last night, the path that the roebuck lies in.

He looks around slowly now.

Gradually he seems to calm down. He talks to himself, but I cannot hear his words. The flowers catch his attention—the flowers that have come open since yesterday. So many of them.

He dismounts and goes to my rose garden, to the very spot where I pray, my own *belaq*. He puts out his hands, as though caressing the air around the blossoms.

This man understands a *gule sourkh*—a rose.

He breaks off a whole branch.

I leap from the window without thought.

The man screams, clasping the roses to his chest. He runs toward the castle door, then seems to think better of it—for a lion has just emerged from the window of that castle. He runs along the outer wall.

I corner him. We must talk. I must make him understand.

He faces me, his cheeks as dark as the roses, his eyes huge and empty.

I take my wide paw and scratch awkwardly in the damp earth. He watches intently. I write, *"Mes roses"*—my roses. What else can I say?

The man looks at the words, tilting his head to read them. He stares at me. "My lord," he says at last.

He has recognized my spirit. I was right to take the chance. I'm so grateful, I pant.

He holds the roses high to cover his face. "Don't kill me," he cries out, "please, don't kill me."

Kill him? O Merciful One, where has your mercy gone?

"My lord," he says again, trembling, peering out through the roses. His eyes dart back to the horse, and I'm sure his pistol is tucked in that saddlebag.

I scratch out French words in the dirt with my paw: "Talk with me?"

The man stares at the words. He looks across to where the roebuck lies. "We can talk of the hunt. You are clearly a great hunter. My lord." His voice is light, but it cannot hide his terror.

I cringe at the false flattery. "Call me Beast." I

stand by the words I've scratched in the dirt. I add, "Rose-thief," and watch his face. Will he catch the irony? Will he realize that no true beast tends a rose garden? Will he rush to apologize?

He drops the roses and shakes his head. "Beast," he says haltingly, "I didn't mean to offend you by gathering these roses. My daughter asked me for one. A little gift for her, that's all. These things happen when a man has children."

This man is thickheaded, after all. Thickheaded, yet blessed with a family. Children. I remember the cubs in the cave. I write, "How many?"

"How many daughters? Is that what you mean? Three daughters, all of whom depend on me." His voice rings with hope. He still believes that I would kill him; he wants this pronouncement to wake my sense of mercy.

Wretched man, who doesn't realize that a true beast has no sense of mercy. Wretched and lucky man, who has three daughters.

He rubs his hands together nervously. "This daughter," he says, "this one who asked for the rose, she's a little goose. She doesn't understand anything." He wrings his hands. "I don't want to die. Oh, Beast, I don't want to die."

He's the goose, the daughter isn't. He understands nothing. But she wanted a rose.

The blood beats in my forehead. I am dizzy for a moment, as the significance of the situation gradually seeps through. This man has a daughter who wanted a rose—who loves roses.

"How old?" I write.

He blinks at the words in the dirt, as though trying to comprehend them. "She's my youngest," he says at last. "A mere child. She didn't know what she asked for. She didn't mean anything by it. I didn't mean anything by it. Please believe me, Beast. I don't want to die. Please, please, don't kill me." He falls to his knees. His eyes are dull behind the tears. "Whatever demonic powers you possess, have pity on me, a mere mortal. I meant no harm, no harm."

Explaining to this man would be pointless; he would never understand. My spirit, which rose so high with optimism just a moment ago, flags once more.

But then I realize I don't have to explain. No. The man has already given me license—for he believes I have powers beyond a mortal. Let that belief be strong. I scratch in the dirt as fast as I can, "Won't die."

His eyes come alive.

I add for effect, "Family won't die."

His eyes bulge. He had not thought of his family dying before.

"If," I write in large, deep letters, "you bring her."

He shakes his head, mouth open. He looks as though he would protest.

I won't give him that chance. I want the daughter who wanted the rose. I write, "I demand."

The man goes white, immobile as pottery. If I pushed him over, his head would shatter. He emits a little scream. His head shakes again. Spittle flies onto his cheek. His terror moves me.

But I cannot afford to know his fears. I have my own needs. Something brought this man to my castle; something offers me a chance—and I've waited so long for this chance. I roar.

He flattens himself on the ground, hands over his ears. Now he's mumbling, "I swear, I swear, I swear." He rises to his knees again and crosses himself, like in the chapel this morning.

I scratch in the dirt, "In 3 weeks."

"Oui," he breathes, "I swear."

I sit on my haunches and watch him.

It slowly dawns on him that our exchange is complete. He mounts and spurs the horse through the crushed brambles, and is gone.

CHAPTER FIFTEEN

Larder

The man must not come this way often, for he knew nothing of this haunted castle. He probably lives many days' journey from here — probably in the Paris that I hear in his voice. Still, he might travel quickly. I should have told him an exact day to bring the child back here, rather than saying it must be within three weeks. What if she shows up too soon?

What if she doesn't show up at all?

But she will. The man was convinced his whole family would die if she didn't. It was cruel of me to leave him with that thought. But anything less might not have been effective. She will show up.

A human child.

I should have pressed for her exact age. What if she's so small, she cries for her mother at night?

A girl child.

But, oh, a girl child certainly won't know how to read. How will we talk to one another?

If I go on like this, I'll drive myself mad. She's a Christian child. Christians love cats for pets. I'll be the best pet cat she ever imagined. She'll stroke my fur. She'll come to love me. Not in the way the *pari* meant, of course. But with time, that love could mature.

For now it will be enough that she's here. This girl child will stroke my fur.

But not at first. I can't expect too much at first. I'll have to win her trust.

I look around and try to see through a child's eyes. Cold, dirty emptiness. Dismay settles over me. No one would find this castle magical, least of all a child. But I don't know what she'd like. Or how to get it, even if I did know. Still, I can stock the larder for her. I can feed this little girl.

My little girl.

I perform the *wudhu* and pray extra long. Then I eat the roebuck almost completely, leaving a small pile of hooves, bones, teeth. I groom myself and roll onto my back, all four paws in the air. There's no point thinking about food for my child now, for I can do nothing outside these grounds during daylight.

I choose a room for her and clean it thoroughly, first with my paws, then with my tongue.

I nap.

At dusk, I crawl under the brambles and out to the world beyond. My first target is the house with the young men, the louts who were drinking from jugs that time the lovers came to the castle.

Across the meadow, through the woods. There it is. The house stands quiet. I trot along behind the trees at the edge of the field. Yes, five people work together, stopping to talk now and then. Two young men drive plows, pushing them through the dirt with nothing but their own brute strength. A third young man, an older man, and a woman follow with shovels and a pick, breaking the overturned clumps. They are like the man who woke in my castle this morning and declared that spring had come. I hope they're right. I want the earth all alive and growing, warm under the feet of my little girl when she comes.

I run back to the house and enter through an open window. The larder first, naturally. A large barrel sits on the floor. I knock off the lid. A few scoopfuls of mixed dried beans lie in the bottom. A wooden box next to it holds a scattering of dried fruits. Another box is a quarter full of ground wheat. This family needed an early spring or they'd have gone hungry. No wonder they're working into the evening like this.

I won't take their food, even if I could figure out a way to carry it off. Anyhow, who eats dried beans in spring and summer? It's time for fresh foods.

Someone's coming.

I leap from the window and away into the trees.

The woman goes into the house. She runs back outside and looks around. She circles the house. Then she goes inside again.

I wait until the men have gone inside, as well. Then I walk over to the shed. The plows, shovels, and pick lean against a wall. Bags of seed are stacked on top of each other. Wheat. These people grow wheat.

All the way home, I'm planning.

I drop a pebble on the front doorstep. Every day I will drop a single pebble here. That way I can know for sure when three weeks have passed.

It takes only a couple of days for me to prepare a large patch of ground for a vegetable garden to the east side of the castle. My claws dig easily, for the heating earth is rich and loose, yet still wet. The weather has definitely changed; snow is unthinkable. These days we have a predawn drizzle almost without fail, just as we did last autumn—a natural watering of the gardens, perfect for roses, which love a damp ground.

At night I scavenge. Most country people have small vegetable gardens beside their homes—gardens they spend the day preparing for seed. I wear a fancy purse around my neck. I found it in a bureau in the bedroom where I sleep. When I come across bags of vegetable seeds, I take a huge biteful out of the bag and spit it into my purse. The seeds stick to my tongue, and sometimes it takes hours to get the last of them off. But I don't care. The only time it was really awful was when I bit into a bag of onion sets.

By day I plant lettuce, cabbage, and those onions. Then carrots, chicory, peas, and so many other vegetables. By the end of a week, the entire garden is planted and fertilized with droppings from the dovecote.

But not everything can be snatched at night from sheds. I want flour for bread. And olives. And olive oil. I want sugar and honey. Everything that's in a well-stocked larder at home, that's what should be in the castle larder when my child comes. Right now the larder's contents are wormy or so dried out, they're hard as rock.

I pass a few days lurking around farmhouses. But it seems there's always someone home—women cooking or looking after children. And I don't dare enter a home larder in the dark—with sleepers in the next room and guns under their beds.

There's no choice: I must go into a village at night and raid the stores.

The risk is great. So I can't take a mere purse worth of goods—I have to take as much as I can manage. In addition to the purse, I bring my blanket, the one I sleep on.

The night is dark. I run along the road. My eyes and

ears alert me to travelers long before they have a chance to see me. I get off into the underbrush on the side of the road and crouch until they pass. Then I run again. The next traveler is a lone man, on foot, and quiet. I duck into the underbrush, but it's clear he saw something, for he moves to the other side of the road to pass and looks back over his shoulder warily. It's all right, though. For if he saw me, he must think he's had a vision. No one would believe a lion roams these parts.

Still, I wish there were more trees here. It's almost as though someone cleared away the surrounding trees, so that the town could be seen from a distance.

Town is nothing more than a few streets crisscrossing with a cluster of buildings attached to one another on both sides. Most of the buildings are two stories tall. Candles flicker from some of the upstairs windows. I understand immediately: The shops are below; the owners live above.

My nose leads me to the baker's first. I spread the blanket on the ground behind the shop. The door is locked. The downstairs windows are shuttered. But the lower story extends to the rear farther than the upper story. I leap onto the roof of the lower story. A chimney pokes up on one side. It's not hot anymore. I look down inside it. There's nothing to see.

I pace on the little roof. Light snores come from the upper window.

I climb onto the chimney and lower myself, all fours against one wall of the inside of the chimney and my back against the opposite wall. The chimney is so narrow, my chest presses against my legs. I stretch out my hind paws, lose the tension that's holding me in place, and fall with a crash.

People call to one another. They come clattering down the stairs. They look around the bakery, searching for an intruder. I am curled in the bottom of the chimney, at the rear of what I realize is the oven. The soot that puffed up around me when I landed now settles in a fine layer that makes me need to sneeze. I press my muzzle against the rear wall of the chimney and pray to the Merciful One to hold back this impulse.

The voices are worried, two of them—a man and a woman. They speculate about the source of the noise.

I need to sneeze. Frantic, I lick a clump of ashes into my mouth. The taste and texture revolt me. The urge to sneeze dies; the urge to purge comes.

The man and woman convince each other that the noise they heard couldn't have come from within their bakery after all. They return to their beds upstairs.

I vomit. In this small space, I can't get away from the scent. But I dirtied my own forelegs, anyway. The scent clings to me.

After a long while I get up the nerve to push

against the oven door. I creep out onto the bakery floor. Barrels of flour and sugar stand beside a large counter. Under the counter are sacks of more flour, more sugar. And there's a large box of coarse powder; my nose tells me it's yeast.

I drag a sack of flour to the door, then a sack of sugar. I spit a mouthful of yeast into my purse.

Something clatters in the alley.

A cock crows.

The night is almost past. The village will come awake within the hour.

And a baker's job begins before dawn.

I go to unlock the door.

The keyhole is empty. The key should be sticking out on this side of the door, but it's not there. I search the floor. No key. I walk around the room, scanning the walls for hooks that a key might hang from. Nothing.

The shutters have two horizonal bars across the inside. They have to be pulled downward at the outer ends, so that they go to the vertical simultaneously. I balance on my hind feet and tap both front paws at the outer ends of the bars. They swing vertical, and the shutters open.

I bite into the sack of flour and drag it between my forelegs to the window. The cloth catches on a splinter in the floorboards. I yank it free and jump onto the window ledge. The sack drops out the window in a billow of white. I jump back inside for the sack of sugar.

Someone walks around upstairs.

Flour and yeast are enough for bread.

But a child needs sugar.

I drag the sugar sack to the window.

It has begun to rain — slow, misty rain, but enough to make my flour clump.

Someone comes down the stairs, clopping wooden shoes.

I jump onto the window ledge and drop the sugar on the flour sack. I leap out the window.

My blanket waits undisturbed. I pull the sacks onto the blanket, then gather the four corners in my mouth.

"Ahhhh!" A woman stands at the open shutters, her hands in the air, her fingers spread.

I stare at her.

She pulls the shutters shut with a loud slap of wood on wood.

I lug the blanket down the alley through rain that's coming harder now. A cat jumps out of my path with a screech. It ducks into an old broken barrel and out the other side. It disappears into a garbage heap.

Without a second thought, I push my blanket into the barrel, shoving the ends with my head. Then I run for the garbage heap.

A dog comes yapping at me. I growl low. He turns tail with a high-pitched scream and races off.

I dig myself into the garbage heap.

CHAPTER SIXTEEN

Candles

I lie under the pile of rubble and dirty old clothes and junk. This is it. I'm finally caught, finally killed.

I tense up, ready to bolt.

Nothing happens.

I wait. Stupid me. I should have run down the road, all the way to the woods. I had time. But who knew? Who knew the baker wouldn't come running with a gun?

Should I make a dash for it now?

A crier's voice starts up: *"Une bête! Une bête horrible!"* He's walking through the streets, warning of a terrible beast that attacked the baker's wife, a beast that almost killed her.

Now his voice is lost in the sound of wheels and horse hooves, people calling to one another, dogs.

Something runs across my back, tunneling between

my body and the garbage cover. Another. Rats. They run over me as though I'm a dead thing. One bites my ear. I give a quiet snarl. It tunnels away, only to return and sniff around my whiskers.

I could open my mouth and make a snack of him.

But someone might just happen to be looking this way. Someone might see the garbage pile heave.

The crier comes by again. The baker's wife has made special buns in the shape of the great marauding beast. They're selling fast. Everyone should hurry, he says, hurry to get one before they're gone.

The baker's wife is no fool. Perhaps the popularity of these buns will make up for the loss of the flour and sugar I stole.

A man yells at a boy. The boy's trying to appease him. They're closer now. A dog barks throughout their talk. The man yells at the dog now. I hear a thump. The dog squeals.

Clatter. They're dumping junk onto the garbage pile. Something sharp pokes me in the shoulder.

The dog whines.

The man and boy walk off, but the dog stays, barking louder and more frenzied. I'm afraid to growl—I don't know who else might be near. The man comes back, calls the dog names. Thump. The dog cries out. They leave.

The rest of the day passes slowly, but without

incident. When night finally comes, I stand up, letting the debris fall off me. I try to pull my blanket from the barrel, but it's stuck fast. I push the barrel with my nose. It rolls on the dirt road with a soft clacking sound.

Whenever the road goes downhill, the barrel flies along and I can trot at close to my normal pace. But uphill is slow. It takes hours to get to the spot on the road below my castle. I clamp my jaws around the lip of the barrel and drag it, walking backward up the hill. When I have the barrel safely inside the castle, I tug at the blanket. It rips, but the sugar sack comes forward enough in the process that I can now bite into it and drag it into the larder. The flour sack comes easily after that. I dump the contents of my purse on the counter—a nice pile of yeast. And nothing got damaged by the dawn rain; the barrel did double duty.

I'm filthy and I reek. I go outside and plunge into the moat, twisting over and over in the water until I feel free and clean again. Then I get out and pray.

The sun comes up, a shiny ball of light. My child needs light. The castle is too dark at night for a little girl. I check the oil lamp. The oil is low. And there's so little oil in the larder.

But I'm through with raiding shops in town.

There are valuables in this castle—carved picture frames, gilded mirrors, fine dinnerware. The child can trade them in town for whatever she needs.

Still, I can't let her arrive to find darkness. I remember the last time I saw my room in Tabriz, my parents wrapped in each other's arms, candles and roses and incense lining the perimeter of the room. And honey-almond balls. Everything ready to greet me.

Incense is foreign to this country. But I can find the rest. I can greet my child properly.

I close my eyes to the sun, and sleep. When I wake, I'm invigorated. Crawling under the brambles excites me. Trotting through the woods excites me. The world feels fresh and bright and firm and mine.

The forest gets thicker to the north. My ears stand stiff. My eyes scan for dead trees. It takes the full afternoon, but finally I hear the buzz. Now the scent of honey comes strong.

There must be a strategy to raiding beehives—for the honey badger does it all the time. But I don't know it. I plunge into the midst of the bees, stand on my hind paws, and swipe my right front paw inside the hole high up in the tree. Bees sting my nose, my ears, my eyelids. I swipe and swipe until my claws catch on the hive. It comes free and falls inside the hollow tree. The bees are crazy now, stinging like mad. But I'm digging furiously at the roots, digging my way under the tree and into its middle. My front paws and head and shoulders are inside the tree now. The bees sting my belly and scrotum from one side, my lips from the other. With my paw I push the hive into my huge mouth. Then I back out and run for the castle.

Bees are inside my mouth. They sting my tongue, the roof of my mouth, the back of my throat.

I dive into the moat and swim underwater as far as I can. When I come up, there are no bees in the air. I open my mouth and drop the hive on the ground beside the moat. A few bees crawl on it still. One manages to fly away. I let myself fall back into the water and I drink and drink, my mouth and head and underside on fire from the bee poison.

I lie all night, all the next day, all the next night in swollen pain.

The poison finally runs its course, and I wake ferocious with hunger. It's morning, and the urge to prowl invigorates me. I put the beehive on the table in the castle and go hunting.

I want a deer, a stag large enough to make me full for days. But what my ears detect is the small yipping of fox kits. I crouch and move low through the underbrush.

A vixen has made a den in the side of a small hillock. She lies curled, half asleep half awake. Two kits locked in mock battle roll in the grasses in front of the den. The father must be out hunting.

I creep up and lunge for the mother.

She has no chance. A single yelp, and I've torn her

throat. The kits race away. I run after them and kill them both. I bring them back and lie in front of the den, feeding. When I finish, I stand and stretch.

What it is that makes me poke my muzzle inside the den, I don't know. It's much deeper than I expected. I crawl forward on my belly. A runt kit presses itself against the back wall and stares at me. I close my mouth around its body, holding it gently. It doesn't fight.

I trot home. The kit is old enough to eat meat. If I can keep it alive, it will make a nice present for my child. She'll laugh at its tiny paws, its fluffy tail. If I can't keep it alive, I'll eat it.

I carry it upstairs to the bedroom I sleep in and put it in the center of the floor. It lies unmoving. But its chest rises and falls. Sly little thing, who thinks he can play dead.

I go outside and spend the rest of the evening chasing quail to discover their nests in the underbrush. I pick up an entire nest in my mouth and carry it home, then go out for another. I gather a total of four nests. Then I go upstairs with two eggs in my mouth.

The fox kit hides. My nose tells me he's under the bed. I drop the two eggs on the floor. They crack; goo oozes out.

I lie down and rest, my paws crossed, my chin on my paws.

The fox comes out slowly. He looks at me. He lifts his nose and sniffs hard. Then he slinks over to the eggs and laps them up.

I stand.

The fox runs under the bed.

I lick the floor clean, for my child will be here soon. I walk out of the room, down the staircase.

The fox follows at a distance. But when he comes to the stairs, he stops.

I remember how hard it was to learn to descend these stairs on all fours. His legs are short; he won't learn soon.

I go to the front step and count the pebbles. It's been precisely two weeks since the man was here. In the next week, that fox kit won't grow enough to learn how to get down the stairs. So I have plenty of time to tame him, befriend him.

A week.

If the man keeps his promise.

But he has to. He believes he bargained for the lives of his entire family. No one would turn his back on such a bargain—not with a beast who scratches words in the dirt.

He must keep his promise.

That night I enter a farmhouse as everyone sleeps. Crazy behavior, I know. But this farm grows almonds, and I want to offer my child almonds with her honey. The trees are just in bloom, of course, but I'm sure the family has nuts from last season in their larder. And this is a fine farmhouse, made of stone, with the bedrooms upstairs. They won't hear me.

I come in through a window and cross a large room into a kitchen. The larder door is shut. I extend my claws and catch the bottom edge of the door and pull it open. Everything anyone could want fills the space: jugs of oil, dried meats, spices and onions hanging from the rafters, and so many nuts. I bite into a large sack of nuts and carry it to the window. With a swing of my head, I toss it outside. Then I jump out after it.

"Who's there?" comes a rough voice.

There's hardly any moon at all; he can't see me. I pick up the sack in my mouth and trot toward the woods.

"Thief!"

Bang!

I run.

Bang!

My whole backside stings. I run as fast as I can, all the way to the castle. I drop the nuts on the floor and go upstairs to the bedroom. I collapse with a groan.

After awhile, the little fox comes out. He sniffs at my backside.

I sit up.

He races back under the bed.

I bite at a painful spot. A lead pellet pops into my mouth. I drop it on the floor with a snarl. I bite another spot, get out another pellet. Then I stop and pant.

The fox comes out. He sniffs at the open wounds. He licks.

Two more spots hurt. I bite out another pellet easily, but the last one is deeper. I have to chew hard for it to come. Then I lie back while the fox licks and licks, until the blood stops.

I fall asleep on my side.

When I wake, the fox kit is curled between my forelegs. The creature has little instinct for natural enemies. I yawn and stretch. The fox runs under the bed.

I'm surprised to find that my backside hardly hurts at all. Nevertheless, I know I was lucky.

Men are dangerous.

I won't go inside any more homes.

Still, the most important thing of all is lacking: candles.

I perform the *wuдhu* and say my prayers. Then I hunt down an old stoat, easy prey. I bring it back to the fox kit and we feed, side by side, him eating the innards, me eating the rest. I lick the floor clean.

For the next few days I wander, lurking near farmhouses and even at the edge of town. I am close to giving up, when I come across a farmhouse that has a set of several beehives. Sure enough, out back of the farmhouse is a vat with a stick on either side and a string running between them over the vat. The vat sits on a stone oven. O Merciful One, maybe this is it. I lie in wait under bushes.

The farmer, his wife, and two sons work in the fields all day. A daughter stays home, keeping watch over three younger children. She sits in the shade and sews while they play. She plucks the feathers off guinea fowl. She cooks. She works all day, but never goes near the vat.

I snooze, counting on my nose and ears to wake me if there's a change. This new routine of going out more by day than night wears on me. But it's good to get used to it. After all, my child will have such a routine.

The rest of the family comes home noisily at dusk to eat.

I run back to the castle, killing two mice on the way. I drop one in front of the kit and swallow the other.

The fox kit chews with little growls. I remember the lion cubs. Will my little girl make noises when she eats? Children do that, often children do.

The next day I'm back under the bushes watching the farmer's daughter. She builds a fire in the pit oven under the vat. She ties several strings to the long string that runs between the two sticks high over the vat. Each of the little strings she adds is weighted down with a stone that dangles at the bottom. She slips her fingers under the loops that hold the top string to the sticks and lifts it free. Then she lowers that top string so that all the dangling strings dip into the vat at once. She raises it again, and hot beeswax drips off each of the little strings. She dips again, then loops the top string in place over the two side sticks and goes inside for a while.

Intermittently throughout the day she dips the strings into the vat of hot wax, building up the layers. By afternoon a row of fat candles swing from the top string.

The younger children play inside and out all day. Finally, a point comes when all are inside. I spring out from the bushes, hook one loop of the top string over my bottom canine, hook the other loop over my other bottom canine, and trot off, with a necklace of candlesticks flopping against my chest.

At home I bite each candle free from the top string.

Tomorrow my child comes. One night to finish my preparations for her arrival, that's all.

And it takes all night to set out bowls with water from the moat and roses floating in them, bowls with bits of honey and almond, bowls with dirt and candlesticks in the center. I arrange them in a semicircle on the floor of the main room.

By dawn, I'm tired. But there's one thing left to do.

My child and her father won't come too early, I'm sure. They can't come while I'm gone. The Merciful One wouldn't allow my plans to be thwarted like that.

I race back to the farmhouse with the beehives out back and the vat of wax. The fire is already lit under the vat. A shotgun is propped against the side of the oven. No candles will be stolen today.

But candles aren't what I'm after.

I run across the farmyard and take a burning stick. I carry it from the end that is just barely warm, walking slowly, so that the fire won't burn out. The family is eating and talking. Soon the farmer and his wife and sons will go out the door. I'm walking too slowly. But every time I break into a trot, the fire wavers and threatens to extinguish.

The voices grow louder.

I trot to the first tree and hide behind it as the people come out of the house. They warn the girl to stay near the vat once the new candles she's going to make today grow thick enough to be of value. The farmer makes her hold the gun a moment.

A curl of smoke goes up from the burning stick in my mouth. O Merciful One, let them not notice.

At last they leave, and the girl goes inside. One small child stays outside, though.

I have to risk it. I walk slowly to the next tree. The child didn't see me. I walk to the next. Then the next.

And now I'm in the woods. I walk slowly, stopping every time the flame weakens.

Finally, I'm home. The fireplace is crowded with the twigs I gathered last night. Beside the fireplace is a stack of branches and logs. I place my burning stick in the middle of the twigs. Flame leaps from twig to twig. I feed it small branches and finally a log.

I need that fire, though the sun has already taken morning chill away from the stone floor of the castle. I need it to light the candles when she comes.

The fox kit cries from upstairs, a mewling sound that he's developed to call me. Foolish little thing.

I lie in the center of the room and sleep.

CHAPTER SEVENTEEN

My Child

Daylight fades, yet the man has not returned. I pace around the bowls on the floor.

The fox cries for me.

I go outside and catch a mouse and bring it to him. But I don't stay beside him as he eats. I have no patience.

I go downstairs and pace again.

A wind comes up, soft at first, then sighing and moaning. Chill returns to the castle.

It's dark now. Would the man come in the dark?

The wind whips around the corners of the castle. Everything creeks.

I count the pebbles again. Twenty-one. It's three weeks. He swore to return within three weeks.

I close all the windows on the first floors. Then I take one candle in my mouth and light it from the fireplace. I use it to light all the others. I replant the first candle into its bowl of dirt. The room seems sealed, remote from the rest of the world. The candles are lonely lights. The roses in the water have opened so fully that the closed air grows rapidly heavy with their perfume.

Let her come. Please.

And I've forgotten my prayers. How can I expect the Merciful One to remember me if I forget Him? I go outside to the moat and perform the *wudhu*. Then I pray.

I hear horse hooves.

This is not the way prayers work. Only children believe that the Merciful One gives gifts directly after prayers. My ears play tricks.

Still, the sound persists. A horse comes snorting through the brambles. A single horse.

Panic strikes. I lope inside and up the stairs.

I hear them talking, calling to each other over the wind, but the words are so hard to catch.

"I can't, Papa." The high voice of the child is stronger than I expected. It rings clear.

A man answers. I know his voice. It is imprinted in my brain forever. He says something about death, something about roses.

"I'm afraid." She cries. "Hold me."

They talk more quietly now. I cannot make out what they say.

The horse gallops away. Were his hoofbeats as

heavy as before? Does he still carry two riders?

I don't dare go downstairs. I won't hasten the end of the shimmering hope that carried me through the past three weeks. I stand at the balustrade, overlooking the front door. The dark of night hides me. The fox kit looks out from behind me. I growl low, and he races back into the bedroom.

There is no noise whatsoever. They have gone. Together. My head is heavy with sadness I have nowhere to pour.

She appears in the open doorway, tall.

A woman.

I lift my head forward.

She steps inside, right foot first, like a Persian bride. Her head is wrapped in a scarf, properly. She stands, looking down.

Her breath comes so lightly, I see no trace of life in her. Is this a vision?

Nothing moves.

Abruptly she turns and, with one swift, decisive pull, she closes the door behind her.

She walks silently forward into the semicircle of candles, kneels over a bowl, and puts her nose to the roses. The small flame dances in the gleam of tears on her cheeks. Her hand emerges from the folds of her skirts, one fine chiseled hand hovering above a bowl of nuts like a hummingbird.

She picks up an almond, dips it in honey, and pulls down her scarf just enough to put the nut in her mouth.

I think of the Greek myth of Persephone, the girl Hades stole to be his wife in the Underworld. She ate six pomegranate seeds, and thus sealed her fate: She had to live with Hades six months of every year — one month for each seed. Does this woman think she's come to marry the King of the Underworld? Is that almond in her mouth a symbol of resignation to a hideous fate? And now I remember Persephone's downfall in the first place: She wandered away from her friends to smell the sweet narcissus. The young woman before me asked for roses. She smells them now. I feel her heart; she believes she is doomed.

She walks the arc of the bowls.

Now she walks under my very feet, O Merciful One, just like a Persian bride. A groom waits on the upper floor as his bride passes under his feet in their new home. Am I a groom? Have I become the monster Hades?

And now I realize the woman has come empty-handed. She carries no baggage. Absolutely nothing.

My tongue dries with the wind of death.

The woman goes from room to room without a word. Then she returns to the chapel, where she stays for a long time. I cannot see her in there; I cannot know if she stands or kneels or bows. If she cries or slaps her forehead on the stone floor or simply talks inside her heart with God.

She comes back to the semicircle of candles. She blows out each one, but the last. She carries the bowl with the last burning candle and comes to the foot of the stairs. She looks up.

The candle illuminates her eyes. What color they are, I may never know, but they are deep and wide. She stares blindly into the dark beyond the little circle of light cast by her candle. She dares to take a step.

I retreat into my bedroom, pushing the door shut.

All the other doors upstairs are closed but one — the one to the room I've prepared for her.

I listen as she comes upstairs, walks the hall into her room, and closes her door.

She's here. My child. My woman.

CHAPTER EIGHTEEN

Belle

I can't sleep. Instead, I spend most of the night in prayer.

By the time my woman wakes, it's full morning. I've already killed a hare, built up the fire, and put fresh roses in the bowls. Sunshine streams in through the open windows.

She comes downstairs, and I leap out the window, to watch from my hiding place.

Her head is bare; her face, naked.

I see the tiny pulse in her slender neck, I hear her soft breath, I smell the parts of her hidden under her frock. She is doelike.

Meat.

The unbidden thought takes me by surprise. Self-loathing steals my breath.

I run for the woods, nausea rising in my throat.

Birds screech. A surprised wolf couple abandons a weasel carcass. I race by without thought, going nowhere, just running. If only I could shed this hateful body. If only I could flee this hateful self.

The land slopes uphill and I lope now, eventually slowing to a trot. I climb until the sun is directly overhead. From this vantage point I can see the land far, far in three directions. No homes. No roads.

I lie down and sleep.

That night I kill a doe. I drink her blood. I eat her hindquarters, then her forequarters, then her head. Only her skeleton remains. I bolted her down in a half hour. My abdomen swells.

After awhile I search for a cave, with no luck. So I sleep in the open. In the warm, gentle rain. The sun comes out, and I sleep all day.

When night comes, I wake. I'm not hungry; I won't be hungry for days. But I'm restless. I wander.

Thoughts come, at last, thoughts of the woman.

I made the man bring her to me—so I did this to myself. I assumed she was a child. What sort of grown woman asks for the gift of a rose from her father? A simple gift if desired by a child; a romantic gift if desired by a woman.

Something stirs in the bareheaded woman. Perhaps she's in love. Perhaps I've ripped her from her lover.

She doesn't smell of a lover, though. How I know

this, I cannot say, but I know it without doubt. Only the slightest twinge of embarrassment at that knowledge interrupts my appraisal of her.

Her face, though naked, isn't ugly. The coarseness of that nakedness shocked me at first. It shouldn't have. After all, I've seen so many women's faces since I left my true home. But the scarf on her head when she entered the castle, the way she walked right foot first, the whole of her demeanor, carried my soul back to sweetest Persia. For one enchanted moment I forgot who she was.

I forgot who I was.

If only she had really been a child, I'd have had a chance, perhaps. Children forgive. What else can they do? But a woman who has been torn from her family, no.

What an insane way to think. My gathering flour and sugar and nuts and candles—all of it was for naught. A castle in disrepair inhabited by a wild beast could never have made a proper home for a child, and it will never make a home for this woman. I am no longer the boy I was when the *pari* cursed me. Hardship has matured me beyond my years. How could I have allowed such self-deception?

This is the fact: A woman lives in my castle. And I thought of her as doelike. I must protect her from myself.

A woman. A bareheaded woman.

But she isn't crude. She simply doesn't know any better. Such is the custom of her people.

And her eyes. I cannot forget her eyes.

The castle is hers now.

My error has cost me dearly, for the castle offered me safety, and a place to retreat into hopeless hopes.

The sound of fast water attracts me. I trot through the woods swiftly. A high river, which I feel sure sinks to a trickle in autumn, like the Zaindeh Rud in my Persia. I dip a paw. The water is as cold as my moat in midwinter. Cold is not my favorite sensation. I wade in. It's deeper than I expected. At the center, I try to swim upstream. The fight stimulates me. I paddle harder, until I give up and let myself be carried downstream and to shore.

I climb onto the bank and sleep.

The next day I meander, in my slow, lion way. I am lion. Prince Orasmyn is no more. See my paws, the tuft on the end of my tail. I rip a gash in my thigh with one swipe of my claws, then I lick the blood. I am lion.

She is a human woman.

With all those qualities that women possess.

What qualities? The only woman I've ever known well is Mother.

This woman has courage. Her closing the door behind herself, smelling the roses, eating the almond—all of it could have been resignation, that's true. But when she climbed the staircase, her eyes spoke courage. She is strong.

But what else do I know of her? Maybe she is not so desirable, after all. Perhaps she has green eyes— my nursemaid Ava would have called that a bad omen. Her head hair is long, just as it should be, it's true, but maybe she is hairy everywhere. After all, her eyebrows are thick. Ava said a bride's facial hair must be pulled out with a folded thread. And a bride must have no hair on her back at the time of marriage. A depilatory of lime and wood ashes and orpiment must be rubbed on her.

On the other hand, if she is hairy everywhere, she is more like a lioness.

And her eyes that stared up into the dark at the top of the staircase were wide set. Those eyes accepted both what they saw and what lay hidden, did they not? For she climbed the staircase. She climbed.

She has a lioness's eyes.

I am trotting. Though I'm not looking for landmarks, though I'm far beyond any landmarks I might recognize, I know I'm heading back to the castle.

At this pace, it takes all day to get home. But daylight lingers long, and I hear laughter from the castle grounds. Laughter.

I crawl through under the brambles.

She's laughing and running, her skirts flying, her sleeves pushed up to the elbow. My fox kit tags at her heels. They've made friends, the two of them, in just two days. She's calling, *"Bête, petite bête, ma chère bête"*—beast, small beast, my dear beast.

The fox has stolen her heart. In a flash, I understand. She thinks he's the beast—the ferocious beast that made her father quake. She's delighted with the surprise.

I lunge from the brambles, bite the fox in the hindquarters, and toss him high. He screams and lands with a slap. He whines pathetically.

The woman shrieks. She stands with both hands in her hair, her face full of horror. Tears stream down her cheeks. She shakes and shakes like a tree in an earthquake.

The fox is quiet now.

I cannot move. I have behaved more terribly than I ever could have imagined. I have behaved bestially. A *qadi*—an Islamic judge—would condemn me.

The only sounds are the woman's sobs. Her hands come down from her hair and now she hugs herself, rocking from the hips. Slowly, ever more slowly.

At last she stands still. Her hands drop and hang limp by her sides. The tears still fall, but her chest heaves less. She doesn't take her eyes from me, though they glitter with fear. She doesn't run.

I walk to the fox kit. He should be meat to me. The woman should be meat to me. I am lion.

The kit's breath comes hard. His eyes are open, but he doesn't seem to see anything. I did this.

The gash in his rump bleeds profusely. I lick it as softly as my tongue will allow. If only his backbone isn't broken. . . .

He mews.

The blood finally stops flowing. I lick his back now, his tiny, pointed head.

His eyes close. But his chest moves fast and rhythmically.

Little fox, I say inside my head. The part of me that knows you as more than meat, the being I was, that part is sorry. I press my nose against his soft belly.

"I didn't know," says the woman, her words broken like bones. "I didn't know he belonged to you. Forgive me."

I lie down beside the kit and stare at the woman. Is she trying to fool me into thinking she knows I am more than beast? And after this awful display?

She looks back at the house briefly, then turns to me with a small shudder. She pulls her sleeves down, smoothing them over her wrists, as though for modesty's sake. She kneels and comes forward, walking on her knees. "I am neither thief, nor seductress." She sits back on her heels and lets her head fall forward until her forehead touches the ground in a perfect *rakat*. She speaks to the earth: "Forgive me. For the love of God, forgive me."

The mix of fear and sadness in her voice matches my heart. If she is duplicitous, she is skilled indeed. I force a puff of air through my lips.

She looks up, into my eyes. Then she comes forward on her knees again, until she reaches the fox kit. She pets it tenderly, her hand coming close to my paw. So close.

I want her to reach out for me.

I want to reach for her.

I jump up and back away. I scratch in the dirt, "You are brave."

She gives a small gasp of amazement and stares at my words. "I don't have a choice."

I wince. "And honest." The tears still cling to her cheeks. Would that I could cry. "I, too, am sad."

"I know. I hear it in your eyes."

She listens to eyes, like my mother does.

My thoughts unravel. Confusion makes me wary. This is a stranger, not my mother, not anyone I understand, not anyone who understands me.

She gets to her feet and curtsies. "My name is Belle."

Belle. The word sounds like the start of *belaq*—a sacred garden.

"And you?" she asks.

The image of Zanejadu replaces that of Belle. I'm startled, then fascinated. Lust rises within me, loosens my tongue. I want to answer her, to tell my whole story.

But a cold wind freezes the well in my heart. I shiver with clarity: The _pari_ wanted me to tell all to this woman. I don't know why, but I'm sure of this. If I am to know this woman, it must be as the lion I have become, not as the prince I once was. Thanks be to the Merciful One, who rules the weather of the heart. "No questions," I scratch in the dirt.

"But I have so many," she says.

I walk away.

CHAPTER NINETEEN

Deer

We fall into a routine quickly. I hunt in the predawn mist. Belle takes a rabbit thigh or half a quail breast and roasts it, leaving the rest of the raw carcass for Chou Chou, as she has named the fox kit, and for me, whom she has taken to calling Mon Ami—my friend—a wishful name, to be sure.

Chou Chou eats his portion on the floor, under Belle's table. I carry mine away to eat in the privacy of the woods.

Chou Chou doesn't seem to understand that I'm the one who caused his limp. He's not a sly fox, after all. He's a foolish, happy little thing. He tags at Belle's heels all day, then curls up against me at night. Despite his wobbly leg, he's learned to maneuver the staircase. The castle and its grounds form one giant, safe den. He's Belle's pet, my cub.

After breakfast Belle tends the vegetable garden. Though her very presence here is due to a request for roses, she has paid no attention to the rose garden, or any of the flowers. Instead, she demonstrates an entirely practical attitude about the things that grow from the earth. She plants all the seeds I bring her, and many yield already under her care. She eats lettuce and peas at noon, lentils and turnips at night. I never watch her eat, though I look carefully as she prepares her plate.

She bakes bread with minced onion and sorrel rolled into the dough. The smell makes my nose wrinkle with interest, but the first time she offered me a slice, I backed away. She doesn't realize a slice is nothing to my gullet; I could eat a loaf in one bite. And she doesn't seem to understand that exciting my palate carries danger—danger I never forget after my outburst against the fox kit.

Or she gives no hint of understanding.

Still, since then, she hasn't offered spiced bread.

But she also bakes small cakes with flour and sugar and dove eggs, from the dovecote. She drizzles honey on top and tucks almonds into the dough here and there. She puts them on a plate on the table, which I easily reach, standing on all fours. For Chou Chou she breaks off chunks and puts them on the floor. I wait until her back is turned, then I eat the cakes. Whole.

The last mistress of this castle must have been close to Belle's size, for Belle has appeared in a number of different frocks. Yesterday I caught her looking at herself in the mirror over her dressing table, turning to the side, as if to admire her profile. When she saw me, she flushed and shut the door in my face.

If she fears me, she gives no evidence. She never asks permission, never apologizes.

Indeed, Belle never talks to me except to say her name for me — Mon Ami — when I perform a task for her or when she offers a cake. Perhaps she interpreted my ban on questions as a ban on her speaking to me entirely. But she chatters to Chou Chou nonstop. I eavesdrop shamelessly, even though it makes me feel like a thief, for I am famished for spoken language. Belle talks about the sky and what weather she can read from it — though she's quite poor at forecasts. She talks about her vegetable garden. About the birds and butterflies that have come in profusion to the flower gardens. About all the details of the world around her. But never about anything else, anything that would reveal who she is. It's as though she exists only as a creature of this moment: without either memories or hopes.

She alternates between being cheerful and being diligent.

She is almost uninteresting.

Perhaps I am becoming a master of self-deceit, to think such a thing. When Belle is near, I cannot take my eyes from her. I know I am in a state of *muraquibah* — guarding. I never touch her, not even the slightest brush in passing. I do all I can to keep evil thoughts at bay.

I am searching my soul for other points of self-deceit as I return from the hunt this morning. It's easy to think now, for I'm not even winded. The kill was quick. Within minutes of my passing through the perimeter brambles, an old wolf practically leaped into my jaws. I drag the body to the front steps before the sun has fully risen.

Belle sits at the table writing. I've never seen her write before.

My ears stiffen, my body goes alert — as when I've sighted a prey. I pad to her side.

She turns with a start. In Belle's hand is a sharp piece of charcoal.

The book is Chinese. Tiny, carefully formed French script fills the generous margins. I read eagerly.

Belle slaps the book shut. "I pray this is not one of your favorite books." She hesitates. "Mon Ami."

The thrill of her speaking to me again after more than two months scrambles my thoughts. I let out a small, rolling growl.

Chou Chou comes cascading down the stairs. He

circles us both, then walks under me, positioning himself between my forelegs.

I sit on my haunches and look at Belle. Chou Chou mimics me. He wags his tail tentatively against my belly.

Belle lays the piece of charcoal on the table and folds her hands in her lap. But her actions are not demure. Her eyes are hard. Her jaw is set.

This is a showdown.

Her audacity interests me. The book must be important. I nudge it with my muzzle.

Belle places her hands, one on top of the other, on the cover of the book. Her cheeks darken. "Will you take this, too?" Anger roughens her voice.

This is a Belle I have not seen before. All my senses sharpen; my breath and heartbeat quicken.

She shakes her head. Her eyes shine. "This is all that's left of me."

All that's left of her, on the pages of a book.

I jump to my paws and race upstairs. From the corner of my bedroom I take *Gulistan* and leap down the stairs as fast as I can.

Belle sits at the table, unmoving. I drop the book in her lap.

Belle looks from the book to me and back again. Finally, she opens it gingerly, turns the pages slowly. She lets her fingers touch the letters, as though reading them with her skin. She lingers over the illustrations. Then she looks at me quickly. "Is this your land?" Her words come fast and stabbing.

I am uncertain as to whether I should answer. But I feel no tremble, no warning from the Merciful One. I nod.

"What brought you here?"

This I know I cannot answer.

She sits taller, her body rigid. She plucks the soft cloth of her sleeve. "What happened to the woman who wore this frock?"

I shake my head.

"You don't know? Or you won't tell? Which is it?" Her questions are a demand.

Their import suddenly dawns on me. What torturous fears rattle in this woman's chest. I knock the charcoal off the table with a swipe. Then I push it under the pad of my forepaw to form words on the stone floor: "Never met."

Belle's eyelids soften and lower just the slightest. I am overcome by the expressiveness of those eyes. I was right—they are the eyes of a lioness.

She pages through *Gulistan,* studying the pictures, all the way to the end. She closes the book and sets it on the table. "There are no beasts in your book."

I write, "People."

"People." She stares at the words on the floor. "People," she whispers. "You care about people?"

I rest my cheek on the cover of *Gulistan.* Then I roll my head until my forehead presses on the cover. I keep rolling my head until my other cheek presses there.

Now I hold my head over the cover of the Chinese book.

Belle watches me.

We both know I can take the book if I want to.

I step back.

Belle's mouth is open. Her face is sad. She extends her hand toward me.

I back up farther.

She leaves her hand in the air for a moment, then picks up the Chinese book. She pauses, seemingly confused. Her eyelids flutter. "This is mine. Whatever else you understand or don't understand, you know that." She rises and carries her book upstairs to her room.

My head swirls. I can't think. I walk to the wolf carcass, rip off a hindquarter, and run to the brambles. I press myself under them and feed, then nap.

When I wake, the weak sunlight filtering through the brambles announces early evening. Crickets sing. I turn my ears until I hear Belle and Chou Chou. Belle is cleaning the wolf skin in the moat, describing every detail of her work to Chou Chou, who makes little snuffles. I hear him digging, probably wracking havoc in the perennial garden nearby.

I wander lazily over to the moat.

Belle has already stretched out the wolf pelt to dry. She walks past me into the kitchen, avoiding looking directly at me.

I perform the *wudhu* and pray. Then I wander slowly through the rose garden. It is now in full perfume. The pungency gives a headiness that makes me almost lose my balance.

When I turn to go inside, Belle's standing in the doorway. Chou Chou bounds out from behind her and jumps into my face. He licks my muzzle and wags his tail stupidly.

"You offered me your book to read," says Belle evenly. "It is wrong to spurn such a generous offer." She holds out *Gulistan*. "Thank you, but I do not know this script. I cannot read this book."

Her words bring a sudden idea that titillates. I walk to the library and look over my shoulder.

Belle lights an oil lamp and follows me.

With difficulty, I knock the *Aeneid* from its shelf.

Belle picks it up. She puts the lamp on the desk and opens the book.

I sit on my haunches, ready. Chou Chou sits beside me.

Belle reads silently.

I give a humph.

Belle glances at me. Chou Chou cocks his head. Belle goes back to her reading.

I hiss.

Belle looks up quickly. Chou Chou whines. Belle waits a moment, then reads again.

I snarl.

Chou Chou throws himself against my neck and licks my ear.

"What is it?" Belle blinks. "Ah." A slow look of realization crosses Belle's face. She reads again, but now out loud.

I lower my front half and lie with my chin on my paws, ears high.

Belle reads quickly, so much more quickly than I can with my lion eyes. She finishes the entire first book of the epic and closes the covers gently. "Good night, Mon Ami." She stoops and kisses Chou Chou on the top of the head before going into the chapel for her night prayers. Then she climbs the stairs quietly.

Chou Chou looks at me. Belle retiring to her room is our cue to go to our bedroom. But despite the heavy meal in my gut, I'm restless. I've been pacing since Belle closed the book.

Belle read the Latin words with feeling. The tones of her voice were like music. They play again in my head. I stop for a moment and let myself listen to the memory of them over and over.

The little fox presses his nose against my chest. He's sleepy.

I lie down. Chou Chou curls up in the arc of my forepaws and chest. The quiet regularity of his quick breath soothes me until, at last, I, too, close my eyes.

The next day, I stay close, trying not to act like Chou Chou, but unable to let Belle out of my sight. All day long I wonder what the night will bring. My throat is thick with hope. When Belle finally cleans up from her evening meal, lights the oil lamp, and heads for the library, I run past her and wait by the book, as eager as a cub.

Belle reads aloud the second book of the *Aeneid*. She reads of the great battles at the end of the Trojan War, of the death of Achilles, of the madness of Ajax, who turns on his own people and slaughters the flocks and herds of the Greeks, thinking they are soldiers, and then kills himself when he realizes his error. She reads of the huge wooden horse within which the Greeks hide and from which they burst after the Trojans are tricked into pulling it within the city walls. The poem tells a tale of nobility, honor, loyalty, glory. My soul sours.

Belle snaps the book shut and stands. She stamps her foot.

I am jarred out of my reverie. I stare at her.

"Where is the glory in a war that leaves a ruined town, wretched widows, dead babies?" She marches up the stairs to her room and closes the door.

Chou Chou follows her, confused. He yips in the hall.

I feel just as stupid. I pace the upstairs corridor. Chou Chou keeps yipping. Finally, I take him by the scruff of the neck into our bedroom. I lick him until he falls asleep.

For the second night in a row, I lie awake for hours. Mother didn't like the *Shahnameh* because of all the violent scenes.

Belle didn't even go to the chapel for her evening prayers, she was so angry.

This young woman holds more complexity than I had guessed.

The next night I go into the library while Belle's eating and take out a volume of Ovid's poems. When I hear her cleaning up from her meal, I carry the book in my mouth and go to stand behind her.

She turns to me, wiping her hands dry on her skirts. "I won't read it."

I come a step closer and drop the book at her feet.

Belle picks it up, examines the cover. She opens it. Then she lights a lamp and goes into the library. She reads deep into the night, her voice filling the room with melodies.

It takes only four nights to finish Ovid's poems. The morning after we have finished, I carry the *Aeneid* out to the garden, where Belle is working. I scratch in

the dirt, "Skip war." It is essential that Belle agree —
for the third book of the *Aeneid*, the crucial book, still
lies ahead.

Belle looks at the words, hesitates, then laughs.
That night she reads from the *Aeneid* again.

She reads about the Trojan warrior Aeneas, who
with the cunning help of his mother, escapes after the
fall of the city with his father and son, though he loses
his wife. He gathers some men, builds a fleet, and sets
sail, to Thrace, then Crete, then Sicily. Along the way
pestilence and storms beset the fleet. The Harpies
attack, frightful stench-ridden creatures with wings
and claws and hooked beaks. The terrible volcano of
Mount Aetna threatens, as do a hundred cannibal
Cyclops, the worst of whom is the great Polyphemus,
blinded by Odysseus. In the end Juno, the vengeful
queen of the gods, sends a storm so great, it tosses
them south, all the way to Africa. Aeneus wanders
homeless, bewildered and aching.

I love this tale, this *Aeneid*. I remember how I had
thought it was inferior to the *Shahnameh* when I first
began to read it. But now it enthralls me. As Belle
reads, I relive the nights I spent hiding from man and
beast before I finally found this castle. Nights of loss
and desperation. Does Belle have any sense of that?
She reads with true inflection, her voice aching over
the pain, shaking with the fears. Something inside her

responds to the tale. But does she have any idea that the *Aeneid* is the only way I can allow myself to tell her my tale, for no one knows the agony of Aeneas better than I do?

When Belle goes upstairs to her room, Chou Chou and I go to ours, and we sleep well.

As morning comes, I go into the library and look ahead in the *Aeneid*. Before Belle came to this castle, I read the first three books on my own — the books that Belle has now reread to me. But that's as far as I got. There are twelve books in all. I'm wary, though. A spot check suggests the last six books deal heavily with war. Belle may refuse to read. But I can always finish on my own, if I want, even though the absence of her mellow voice will greatly diminish the pleasure.

I go outside, perform the *wudhu*, and pray. Then I prowl. But no hapless creature crosses my path during what must be at least an hour. So I go to the pond. A fat duck would be a nice change.

Several duck families are already in the water. A crow spies me and screeches as he takes to the air. The ducks swim madly, leading their ducklings to the center of the lake. To reach them, I'll have to get thoroughly soaked. And I'm not a fast swimmer — I might never catch anything but the smallest ducklings.

I don't want to think about Belle's reaction to my bringing home a passel of dead ducklings.

I pad along the edge of the pond, grumpy, when I almost step on a late nest full of eggs. I lower my ear to them. There's a quiet inside these eggs; they may be newly laid. The nest is larger than my mouth, so I can't take the whole thing. I rest my chin on the edge of the nest and press down hard. With my right paw, I nudge an egg little by little into my open jaw. Then the second and third and fourth and fifth. There's no room for the sixth. I should have eaten one first. But it's too late now; I won't take the chance of emptying my mouth and possibly cracking an egg.

I trot home. Belle is not downstairs. I go upstairs. Her door is closed, and Chou Chou lies outside, eyes wide and alert. When he sees me, he jumps at my muzzle in greeting.

I sit on my haunches. Chou Chou leaps at my back, tumbling across me, wondering why I won't play with him. I sit here stupid with a mouthful of eggs, waiting for Belle.

Finally, she opens the door. She looks at us with surprise.

I open my jaws wide.

Belle's breath catches. Then she laughs and, oh sad truth, I think I detect relief in that laughter, though I cannot see her face well with my eyes scrunched up from my open jaw.

My jaw wants to close. She's taking her time. Assessing the risk, perhaps?

"Duck eggs. Magnificent." Belle makes a scoop of her skirt and fills it with the eggs from my mouth. She walks down the stairs carefully and puts them on the table.

Then she picks up Chou Chou and nuzzles her face in his neck fur.

Jealousy stings. I look away briefly.

Belle has still never touched me. Just now, as she took the eggs from my mouth, her hand didn't even knock against a tooth.

She cracks an egg into a bowl and puts it on the floor in front of greedy Chou Chou. She pulls teasingly on his tail as he licks at the dark yolk.

She cracks a second egg into a bowl on the table and turns to me, to her other pet—the gigantic, untame one. I am supposed to lap like Chou Chou. Lap before her human eyes.

I back away. Then I turn and run.

I'm in the woods in minutes. I race. And I know this is absurd. I ran away from Belle once before, only to return. This is my life. I cannot escape it. Yet I run. I run full out and wild.

At length I stop and stand, my head hanging. I shut my eyes and work to remember. I search every crevice of my mind. My nursemaid Ava's voice comes to me, with all the rules of my Persian heritage passed from generation to generation:

If you kill an animal at night, you must say, "I am

killing you as well as the one that matches you," so that this animal will not reappear after its death.

If you slit the throat of a fowl, you must say, "In the name of the Merciful One," before eating it.

You must never kill a hen or sheep at sunset.

You must never kill a white cock ever—it's an angel.

All the rules taught to me speak in my head, but they might as well not. I have killed so many animals, morning, noon, and night. Killed without rituals of any sort.

I remember the teachings of the religious *sheikh* who taught me the *Qur'an* day after day, week after week, month after month, until I was finally ready to discuss it with Mother and Father and the *imam*, the prayer leader.

I remember the pillars of my faith. The confession and declaration of faith. Ritualized prayer. Almsgiving. Fasting and contemplation during Ramadhan. Pilgrimage to Mecca and Medina at least once in a lifetime. Good deeds. Protection of Islamic beliefs.

I declared my faith as a child. I made my pilgrimage as a young man. But since I've become lion, the rest of the pillars have crumbled. I pray, but not five times a day—and some days I don't pray at all. I haven't even attempted to observe Ramadhan, for when hunger comes upon me, it comes in a complete way, filling every part of me with need. There is no room for contemplation. I cannot give alms to the poor. Indeed, I steal what I need. I do not perform good deeds. If there are members of Islam in this strange country, I cannot help protect their right to practice their beliefs.

I am lost.

Orasmyn is lost.

But, no. There are five basic principles of my faith. First, there is one Merciful One. Second, the prophet Muhammad is the last in the line of true prophets to present the Merciful One's message to man—a line of prophets that runs from Ibrahim on to Ishmael and Isaac and Jacob and Joseph and Job and Moses and David and Solomon and Jesus and so many. Third, the body and soul are resurrected on Judgment Day. Fourth, your actions will be rewarded or punished by divine justice. Fifth, there were twelve spiritual leaders, successors to Muhammad, who interpreted the inner mysteries of the book of sacred laws, the *Shar-i'ah,* as well as the *Qur'an,* twelve *imamha* free of sin and chosen by the Merciful One through Muhammad.

I believe these principles. Whoever I am, wherever I go, whatever I do, I believe them. Somewhere inside me a soul clings to them.

I must hold fast to these beliefs.

Crack.

I don't move, yet my muscles tighten. Something walks in the forest. I breathe deep: the scent of deer. I open my eyes and slowly turn my head. The fawn still has speckles. Her nose is thick black and shines wet. She's been drinking from the pond. Everything about her is sacrificial.

One lunge.

But the fawn runs to her startled mother.

I race after and bring down the fawn.

The doe leaps away without a backward glance.

I eat. This is my life. This. No amount of reciting principles of faith can change this. I run back to the castle, my stomach churning with so much food.

Belle is in the woods. She leans over a wild caper bush, picking them and dropping them into her skirt, that skirt that held the duck eggs just this morning. Her backside presents itself to me. Like the backside of a lioness.

The urge to mate renders me hot and savage. I stare at her, unmoving. This must pass. Please, Merciful One, stop me. Stop me or kill me.

Belle straightens up, turns, sees me. Her face goes pale.

My own face is smeared with the blood of the fawn. I know that—I didn't clean myself on purpose, just so I could show her this face.

Her eyes flash horror, and she doesn't even know it was a fawn—a baby.

I should tell her, I should tell her it was innocent— and tender and delicious. She should know that whatever lives is meat to me. She should know.

This is how I eat, Belle, this is who I am.

But the ground is hard here and covered with brush — I cannot scratch out the words.

Or am I not only beast, but coward?

"Venez" — come. Belle walks back, taking a path through the brambles that she has obviously cut just this morning. She pours the capers into a pile on the front step. Then she goes to the moat. "Please," she says.

I come forward.

She dips the edge of her skirt in the moat. Then she puts her left hand on one side of my face, as though cupping it.

I tremble at her touch at last.

She feels my tremble. Her eyes grow bright with unshed tears. I would try to understand why, but I'm beyond reason. Her heat comes through her palm. With her other hand she wipes my muzzle clean. Her breath is duck egg and parsley on top of her own private smell.

I breathe in as much of her as I can.

When she has finished, she sighs and stands tall. "I need oil for the lamp and olive oil for eating. What should we do?"

I admire the way she forces us past the moment.

I go inside to the library and pull open a drawer with my teeth. I carry back a valuable silver letter opener to Belle.

She takes it from my mouth, examines it, then looks at me, still as death.

Only now, as I see her stricken face, do I realize another possibility: The letter opener is sharp. If Belle wanted, if she dared, she could stab it through my eye, into my brain. I wait, not knowing whether I offer myself or not. My head is heavy; it wants to fall on the floor.

I have been here before. I offered myself to Father. But I backed away because I knew it would destroy him when he realized he'd killed his son. There is no reason to back away from Belle, though. I wait.

"Ah, I see." She nods slowly. "But how does one get to town to sell this thing?"

So she won't kill me. And now I think of the guns in this house. Has Belle ever considered killing me? Does she believe I can't be killed? Or is such a thought anathema to her? Anger flares in me at her fundamental gentleness. No one should hold that much goodness.

"How?" she says again.

I force my attention to her question. Town is too far for Belle to walk there and back in one day. She'd have to stay overnight.

Would she ever come back?

She watches me. At last she says, "All right. We'll have to think about it. We'll find a way."

CHAPTER TWENTY

I watch the stars. Belle is in her room. Chou Chou whined in ours for a long time, then finally gave up and settled down on the blanket alone.

I roll in the dirt at the edges of the vegetable garden. I scratch the back of my head against a cornerstone of the castle. But nothing calms me. Nothing soothes.

The night is full of creatures. I hear them in the air, in the brush, under the ground.

Belle washed the blood from my whiskers. But the taste remains in my mouth.

I walk to the rose garden and flop down against the thorns. I close my eyes and wait for morning.

Belle opens the front door. She holds Chou Chou to her chest and croons. Then she sets him on the ground.

Chou Chou runs immediately to where I lie under the roses. But he doesn't jump on me. He waits. Almost with patience—a virtue I've never seen a trace of in him before.

I stretch.

Chou Chou's eyes brighten. He jumps on me in uncontained joy. The night all alone must have been very long for him.

We roll together in the dirt, me being careful not to squash him, him being swift to move out of harm's way.

"Mon Ami."

I look up.

Belle still stands in the doorway. She must have been watching us this whole time. She puts the fingertips of both hands lightly to her lips. Everything about her is suspended.

I'm caught in her hesitation, disoriented. I walk to her and sit on my haunches, waiting, just as Chou Chou waited before me only moments ago.

At last she takes a deep breath. "I'd like to show you something." She goes inside.

I follow.

Belle hurries up the stairs and comes down a moment later. In her hand is the Chinese book. "Do you prefer to read on the floor or the table?"

I lower myself to a crouch, hardly breathing.

Belle puts the Chinese book on the floor in front of me. Her eyes close for a moment. When she opens them, her hands also open the cover of the book. I read.

> I am lost. What the beast wants of me, I cannot know. Papa said he promised there would be no deaths if I came. But his jaws reek of blood.

I close my mouth in shame. Belle sucks air between clenched teeth. I can feel her eyes watch me. I smell the sour taint of fear from her body.

Guilt makes lead of my heart. When Belle first came, I managed not to feel sorry for her, because she never complained of loneliness, never spoke of fear. But ever since she asked what happened to the woman whose frocks she wears, I've known what she hides. Yet I don't tell her to leave. I don't reveal that I lack the evil power her father told her I have. I don't tell her I'm not demonic.

The amount of courage it took for her to offer this book to my eyes holds me fast. I don't understand what made her change her mind. But I am grateful for such an enormous gift. I will strive to be worthy of it. I read, reverent.

> He kills me each night in my dreams. I would run away, but that would only hasten the end. For he would catch me, as he catches any

other animal. The only real choice is to kill myself. But God would never forgive that. And so I wait.

As do I, Belle. The *pari* trapped me, and I trapped you. Wretched choice. A prince should know how to make better choices. I turn the page and read.

I fill my days with learning the new skills of gardening. It isn't hard.
Waiting is hard.
Gardening is easy. Not even Adelaide and Felicie could complain if they saw what I have done.

I read, turning the pages with the tip of my tongue. I wish I could read faster, as I did in my old body. I am eager for the secrets in these words. It is as though a flower bud unfolds, petal by petal, before my eyes.

Sometimes a plan will come to me. A way to fool any man, and escape. Hope swells. Then I stop. I am forthright with him because he is a beast. How can you dissemble with a beast?

The words stab me. I want to shut this book and

run. But I cannot. I have to know more. I read while Belle scurries around the kitchen, cutting wolf meat left from yesterday. I read while Chou Chou jumps on me and nips my mane, begging to play more. I read and read.

After the initial pages of shock and despair, Belle writes of her family. Her father is a merchant, as I guessed. She has three brothers and two sisters. Belle is the youngest, because her mother died from a malady following childbirth. They were well-to-do, never wanting. All the children got an education, both in books and in manners. But a couple of years back, the family fell on hard times. Belle's father paid much for several shipments of exotic goods he planned to sell, then the ships were lost at sea. Goods from China and India and, yes, Persia, my Persia.

I look up at Belle. She's rubbing salt into a slab of the wolf meat.

I want to ask her for the list of the goods her father expected in those shipments. I want to hear the words of all the things that used to be familiar to me. To remember their feel and look and smell and taste. To be once again in the crowded bazaar, breathing the sweat of my fellow Persians. To work in the gardens with my friend Kiyumars. To share a meal with Mother and Father.

I grieve inside. My body rocks rhythmically on the

four pads of my paws. I want to scream. I want to scream or cry.

Belle works assiduously, pressing the heel of her hand into the tough meat, over and over. I rock to her rhythm now. The tense angle of her neck tells me she works to keep herself from thinking about me reading her words. How does Belle keep from screaming?

Gradually I calm down. The need to know more seizes me again.

Belle's written words tell of her father in debt, with no means to repay. The family let their servants go and managed from day to day. Her brothers took odd jobs. Belle took over the servants' tasks—cleaning, cooking, sewing, making fires. But her sisters refused to work, complaining that it would reduce their social standing.

Then her father got news that his ships had finally reached port—a southern port, to be sure, but at least the ships were safe. That's why he traveled all this way through largely unpopulated land, all the way from Paris; he couldn't wait for the ships to sail around the south of Spain, through the Strait of Gibraltar, and up to a northern port, closer to home. He had to go to them immediately.

But, though the ships had arrived, much of the cargo had been pirated away. What was left barely paid the crew's wages and the port duties. Belle's father was riding home, a ruined man, when the sudden snowstorm made him lose his way.

The girls had asked him to bring gifts. After all, they expected him to return rich again. Belle's sisters asked for jewelry, fans, ostrich feathers, brocaded frocks, even a monkey.

Belle asked for a rose.

Why? I look up again. But Belle is gone. She and Chou Chou have deserted me. The slant of the sunbeams through the window tells me it's midday already. I hear the two of them near the dovecote.

I hold the questions in my mouth: Why, Belle? Why a rose? Were you in love, Belle? With whom? Do you love him still?

I could go outside and scratch my questions in the dirt. But I stay here, instead. If she has a true love, I don't want to know.

But true love or not, Belle's sisters and brothers treated her as a servant. Her father gave her no protection. She's no worse off here with me than there with them. Maybe she's even better off here.

I shake off this hateful guilt and read again.

Belle's father returned home and told of me. Her brothers said they'd come with guns and kill me. But her father said no one could kill a devil. If he didn't keep the bargain, they'd all perish.

The rest of the pages tell of her fears of me, separated by descriptions of random events. Memories stirred by our evening readings. Escapades of her childhood. I grew up an only child, adored by my parents and adoring them. She grew up plagued by rogue brothers and silly sisters—all of whom she writes about with a fondness that surprises me at first, then irritates.

I close the book and walk outside. On the ground by the front door lies a hindquarter of the wolf. Belle placed it there for my breakfast, unaware that the fawn I ate yesterday will satisfy me for days.

Chou Chou trots beside Belle as they come toward me from the dovecote, a pile of raspberries from the canes surrounding the cote in the scoop of Belle's skirt. I look at Chou Chou's limp, the limp I caused, and my lips curl under. In this moment I cannot bear Belle's solid goodwill. I want to run.

Belle walks past. She glances at me quickly, almost shyly. Her cheeks darken. She pours the berries onto the table. Then she goes to the garden and digs up a leek. She washes it in the moat and carries it inside.

I perform the *wudhu* and pray long. At last I go inside and watch Belle stirring a small pot of soup.

I know this woman now. Or much of her.

The small movements of her back tell me she feels known, and she is flustered by that feeling.

All comfort departs.

She ladles out a bowlful, puts it on the table, and sits. Then she looks at me. And waits.

I have never before stayed there during her meals. I don't want to stay now. But I have to.

Belle blinks, then picks up her spoon. The small silver bowl of the spoon dips into the soup, comes directly to her mouth. She hesitates, but doesn't look at me. I hear her heart—it stops. Then she sips. Over and over. Not a drop spills. This is how a human eats. This is how I once ate.

Belle is human. I am lion. Belle is human. I am lion. Belle is human. I am lion.

The chant rolls in my head.

She hums.

The chant dissipates.

Belle hums as she eats.

Like a lioness.

Is this the work of the *pari,* who distorts every moment, makes every moment a source of temptation?

Belle and I mustn't wait for evening. We must read now. Immediately. We must be brought to the humanity of Aeneas.

I go to the library and fetch the book. I put it on the table beside Belle.

She carries the book outside and sits with her back against the trunk of a fig tree. I lie beside her. It's a hot day, but the ground is cool in the shade of the fig.

Chou Chou's head pops up from a hole in the ground. Dirt covers his snout; he's been digging a tunnel. He jumps out and runs at us, leaping across Belle's frock, tracking dirt everywhere. She shoos him off.

He sees a mole in the grass and races away.

Belle laughs. Then she opens the *Aeneid* and begins the fourth book.

> *At regina gravi iamdudum saucia cura*
> *volnus alit venis et caeco carpitur igni.*

My ears ring as if someone has beaten them. I listen to the story of Queen Dido, who falls in love with Aeneas, in love to the point of distraction. I know that this book will end badly. How can the poet Virgil do this—take us from the raging thirst of battle, to the calm of acceptance, to this twisted misery?

I get to my feet and pace.

Belle looks up, surprised. When our eyes meet, she blushes and looks away. She rips a fig leaf from the tree and uses it to mark our place in the book.

I circle her, wide at first, but now closer, tighter.

"What is it, Mon Ami? What are you telling me?"

I hear her breath quicken as I circle closer.

"Of course," she says softly. "Of course that's the answer. Let's try." She puts the book on the ground and grabs hold of my mane with one hand.

I stop moving. For a moment, my eyes go blind with excitement.

She throws a leg across me and, in an instant, she straddles my back.

Belle rides me. The beauty rides the beast.

I walk the path through the brambles, the path she cut yesterday. Then I trot. She holds fast with both hands.

I run.

CHAPTER TWENTY-ONE

Letters

B elle comes downstairs in the frock she wore when she first came here. She goes into the library.

I watch her from the doorway, impatient. This morning I caught her a fat rabbit. It's her favorite meat. I stole lemons from a nearby orchard, and I broke off a branch of rosemary from a hedge near the road. These things lie on the table like a row of gifts. I want her to see them. I want to watch the happy smile come to her face. I want her to know that I give her gifts, while her family gave her nothing.

Instead, she's in the library. I can't bear to listen to Dido's story now. I refuse to follow Belle into the library.

But Belle doesn't pick up the *Aeneid*. She sits at the desk, smooths a piece of parchment in front of her, and writes.

A note for me? But she can always just talk to me. I wait, curious.

She folds the parchment. Then she takes another piece of parchment, a bit larger, and folds an envelope, slipping the first parchment inside it. She addresses the outside.

Belle has written a letter.

To whom?

I walk away quickly and quietly, outside and around to the window, where I can watch everything she does without risk of being seen.

She picks up the metal stamp and walks into the main room. She goes to the fireplace, lights a candle, drips a bit of wax on the envelope to close it, and presses that stamp into the seal.

Finally her eyes go to the table. She laughs in delight and skins the hare expertly. She calls to Chou Chou, but the little fox has been outside for hours, sleeping in his newly dug den. He's not hungry. I watched him eat a rat that came up from the moat this dawn. The rat was sluggish and old, or Chou Chou never could have caught it. But the fox didn't seem to know that. He swung his catch by the tail and trotted in his uneven gait around me, parading his victory.

Belle calls for me now.

I crouch, to be sure she cannot see me. She stops calling. I slowly stand tall again and watch her.

She skewers the hare whole and leans the skewer against the wall of the fireplace, as far as possible from the hottest part of the fire. I understand: This way, the rabbit will roast slowly. It will be ready by afternoon. Belle must have plans for the morning. Plans that involve that letter.

Belle picks up the silver letter opener, which has been lying on the table since I first brought it to her. She comes outside and finds me. "Ah, here you are at last." She smiles. "Shall we go?" She climbs onto my back.

So this is what I've been reduced to—her means of transportation. No better than a horse.

Or a camel.

The memory of Jumail, the camel I wrongly sacrificed, comes like a bolt of lightning. I flinch.

But the weight of woman on my back overcomes thought. The heat of her legs intoxicates me. I take her out through the woods, across the meadow. We skirt around farmlands, loping easily. At the last stand of woods before town, I stop.

Belle dismounts in tacit agreement. "Do you need me to bring back anything from town?"

Only you, I think.

Belle looks at me a moment more. Then she walks to the road and into town.

I wait, my head full of questions I despise myself for having.

The sun climbs to its zenith. Still, I wait, drifting in and out of sleep. In midafternoon, Belle reappears, thanks be to the Merciful One. She carries a large cloth sack over her shoulder.

I get to my feet.

Belle smiles and climbs on my back.

But I'm thirsty after waiting so long. I stop at a stream.

Belle gets off and looks at me questioningly.

I have never lapped water in her presence. But now that she's seen me with blood on my muzzle, how can anything be worse? I splay my front legs and lower my head.

I can't. I can't drink. I don't want her to see me this way. I look at her.

Belle quickly squats and cups her hands. She fills them with water and puts her face in, drinking noisily. On purpose? Her eyes are closed.

I lap the water.

When I finish, I look at her again.

Belle finally peeks over the edge of her hands and smiles. Then she laughs. She fills her hands again and . . .

SPLASH.

Belle has tossed the water in my face.

I shake my head in surprise.

She watches me, mouth open, breathless. When I

do nothing, she splashes me again and laughs. And again.

I slap my paw in the water and splash her back.

All at once there is water everywhere. A war of splashing and splashing.

Water and woman everywhere. Woman's laughter, light as bells. Woman's hair, hanging in long, silky strands. Woman's hands gleaming in sunlight. Woman's body, warm under clinging wet cloth.

Woman woman woman.

I leap, and knock her to the ground.

Belle lets out a scream.

But I have already stopped, shocked at myself.

She gets to her feet, clutches her arms across her chest, and stands panting, staring at me.

I shake off, and walk away.

Belle runs after me. "Please, Mon Ami. Please."

I stop and look over my shoulder at her. What does this woman, who plays like a child, understand of the world?

But Belle's face is not childlike now. Her eyes hold misery. "I should have known better. It was my fault."

I turn to her in hope. Has she guessed at who I am?

"I'm sorry," says Belle. She takes a step forward. "I know you need my help. I'm so sorry."

I need no one's help. I am Prince Orasmyn. I roar.

Belle straightens at the noise. She clasps one hand in the other. But she doesn't step back.

My roar finally dies from the air.

How foolish to have made such a racket so close to town.

Belle wipes the water from her face. She lifts her sack with a trembling hand. She remounts without a word. We pick our way carefully through the farmland.

Once at home, she immediately assumes a business air. She lays out the treasures from her sack, one by one. Oil for the lamp and olive oil for cooking. But that's not all. No, she has a melon and corn and spices. She has hazelnuts and medlars and cherries. She has olives and bacon and cheese and walnuts. As she puts each thing on the table, she announces it and checks my face for reaction.

She is still shaken by our encounter at the stream, yet she cannot hold back the rising glee she feels at the treasures on the table. It creeps into her voice, stronger with each announcement. The steadfast innocence of Belle would condemn the best of men. And I am far from the best.

She stops, one hand still in the sack. She looks at me and smiles, her lips parted. Slowly she takes out a bottle of red wine. She pulls out the cork and holds it under my nose. "For you," she announces triumphantly. "I will put some in the best bowl."

The smell of the alcohol assails me. I step back and blink.

Belle looks confused. "You don't like it? It's the same wine that I found in the larder, but not rancid."

Belle thinks I'm responsible for everything here. She knows I came from far away, but somehow she hasn't realized this is not my castle. When she reads from the *Aeneid*, she doesn't know the story is mine, as well. The loss of my homeland, of my parents, of my very body—Belle knows nothing of these.

I am alone, but for the Merciful One. I go outside to the moat.

Belle comes alongside me, her face dismayed.

I want to pray.

But Belle stays with me.

Well, I don't care. She can't disturb me; she is totally unrelated to me. I perform the *wudhu* and pray.

When I rise from the first *rakat*, Belle whispers, "Do you pray to your god?"

I scratch in the dirt, "Only one God."

"Yes, you're right. There is only one God." Belle goes to the moat and washes her face and hands. She wets a part down the center of her hair. She washes the tops of her feet. She bends over awkwardly. *"Agnus Dei, qui tollis peccata mundi, miserere nobis,"* she chants, saying the same prayer her father said the night he came to my castle. Then she stands straight and bends again. She does this three times, each time with a prayer.

I am amazed that she knows my prayer ritual so well. I stare.

"I watch you from my window every morning," she says simply.

I realize her bending from the hip in this angular way is her attempt at mimicking the strange way I let myself hang from my shoulder bones when I pray. I crouch now and put my chin on the ground.

Belle studies me. Then she kneels and folds herself down to the ground in a deep bow.

Belle is smart. Smart and brave and good.

"I interrupted you," she says. "Would you like to finish?" She comes very close and leans toward me. "Will you allow me to pray with you?"

And so we pray together, my head hanging low from my shoulder bones, Belle's face to the dirt in a proper *rakat.*

For the next two weeks we enjoy the end of summer, the shortening of the days. We begin the day with Belle writing in her diary, as she calls it, while I hunt. Then she bustles off. She has some sort of project out in the clearing that she won't let me see. She covers it with pine branches when she's not working on it. When I come near, she shoos me away with a laugh. I am curious. But I can wait. It feels good to know that she'll let me in on the secret when she's ready.

But that's not all Belle's busy with. She makes cakes of walnuts and cherries. She gives them dry to Chou Chou, but she drenches mine in honey. She has noticed my fondness for it. I devour these cakes. And Belle never offers me wine again, nor do I smell it on her breath.

We finish the fourth book of the *Aeneid* and start the fifth, reading for less time now, because every night before Belle goes to bed, we pray together, doing our versions of the *rakat* side by side.

We have reached a delicate equilibrium.

At least until today. Today I'm grouchy with hunger. Belle took the rabbit I left her from this morning's hunt and gave none of it to me. None at all. She didn't give any to Chou Chou, either. But she at least gave the little fox chunks of stoat meat from yesterday's hunt. I got nothing.

So I've been wandering about the grounds, tense and twitchy. I could go off and easily kill myself another rabbit. But I don't want to leave. I'm afraid I'll miss out. Something's going to happen; Belle's planning something.

All afternoon she's been working on building a fire in the clearing at the site of her secret. Her pile of pine boughs keeps me from seeing what's going on, but I watched her carry fire logs and I've seen and smelled the curling smoke.

Now, though, there's another smell. Roasting meat. I sniff. It's rabbit. Belle's roasting this morning's rabbit outside. Why?

Belle comes out of the kitchen with three large bowls stacked together. Cabbage and peas sit in the top bowl. She heads for the clearing.

I block her path.

Belle laughs. "I was wondering when your curiosity would win." She laughs again. "All right, Mon Ami, I have a present for you." She puts the stack of bowls on the ground. "First, let's wash and pray."

I'm full of questions, but Belle is already halfway to the moat. We perform the *wudhu* and pray.

After the last *rakat,* she skips ahead of me and picks up the bowls. "Come on." Her smile excites me.

I follow her to the pine brush. She puts down the bowls and clears away the boughs.

A stone hearth holds a white fire with a rabbit roasting on a ledge halfway up.

Belle kneels and arranges the bowls in a row on the ground. "I know Chou Chou won't eat greens." She looks up at me. "And I suspect you won't, either?" Her voice rises in a question.

I nod.

Belle smiles. "Chou Chou," she calls, over her shoulder. She uses tongs to move the rabbit from the hearth to one of the bowls. Then she cuts off a leg and puts it alone in a bowl. She places that bowl in front of Chou Chou, who has come running from his den.

Chou Chou sniffs warily at the cooked meat. He puts his nose to it and jumps back.

Belle laughs. "Let it cool down, little silly." She cuts off a second leg and puts it on top of the greens.

Then she pushes the bowl that holds all the rest of the meat toward me.

I look from the bowl to Belle.

"Please, Mon Ami." Belle sits back on her heels and folds her hands in her lap. "In this hearth I can cook any kind of animal you catch, any size."

Cooked meat. It's been years since I've eaten cooked meat. I remember verse eighteen of book one of Rumi's *Masnavi*:

> State of the cooked is beyond the raw
> The wise in silence gladly withdraw

Belle's instincts are good. But do I even like cooked meat anymore?

Belle's chest rises and falls in heavy breath. "We can enjoy meals together. Please."

Meals together. Meals in which I rip meat with my fangs and crack bones to suck out marrow. This is what Belle wants to share?

"Together," says Belle. "Like friends." Her voice grows firm. "Like a family."

Amazing thought. And verse twenty-one from Rumi's *Divan-e Shams* comes to me now:

> O Shams-e Trabrizi, you
> Compassionately blend and renew
> East and west through and through
> And so we say, may it be so

I am east and Belle is west. Can we be compassionately blended? Can we be family together?

Belle leans toward me. "You don't have to drag your meat into the woods. You don't have to eat behind my back. Please, Mon Ami. Let me help you."

Let Belle help me.

I want to tell her I am the Prince of Persia. I want to say I need no help. I am not weak.

But I want to eat with her at this hearth. I scratch in the dirt, "Thank you."

Belle smiles the most beautiful smile in the world.

I stretch my forepaws out on either side of the bowl and bite into the meat. It is good to eat cooked meat again. Good to eat with company.

We stay long by the heat of the hearth.

When Belle rises, I press my nose against her hand. "What, Mon Ami?"

I lead her to the rose garden.

Belle stops at the border.

I take the hem of her skirt in my mouth and pull her forward.

Belle walks slowly. "It is beautiful, Mon Ami. I thought it was forbidden me, because you got so angry at Papa for taking roses. All this time I've wanted so much to walk here — to enjoy the simple pleasure of a rose." She puts her face into clusters of blossoms over and over. She laughs.

I bask in the purity of Belle's laughter. For the first time since the *pari* cursed me, I am happy.

The next morning Belle comes downstairs in her original frock again. Immediately I know she wants to go to town. I wonder what she will sell, what she will buy. But as far as I can see, she goes empty-handed.

She rides me through the woods, and the whole way I am wondering what she will do in town. Her empty hands worry me.

At the same place as last time, Belle dismounts. She turns and walks away.

I hesitate, then run after her, out in the open, where any passing human might see me. I scratch in the dirt, "Will you come back?"

She says solemnly, "Let your heart tell you." She leaves.

I go back to the woods and wait.

I don't want to wonder how to interpret her words. I want my heart to know. But my heart splutters.

My heart tells me I love Belle.

Crazy heart. I cannot listen to my heart.

Belle returns quickly, her face pinched. She gets on my back, and I feel the squeeze of her thighs. Her fingers dig into my mane.

I run, I run as fast as I can.

When we get to the castle, she slips off and rushes inside. She chops vegetables. Then she comes outside again, her face distracted. She walks swiftly through the flower garden that is all but past. Only the roses are still in form. She goes right to Chou Chou's den, but he's not there. The little fox strays more often and longer every day.

She twirls around and catches me following her.

I pause.

She comes to me. "I don't know what to do." She falls to her knees.

I want to hold her, cradle her. Her sadness is dreadful. I sit on my haunches as close to her as I can get without pressing on her.

"I wrote to Papa. But he doesn't answer. I'm afraid for him. He isn't strong." Belle sighs. "I want to visit him." She looks at me with her wide lioness eyes.

I scratch in the dirt, "You miss that life."

Belle shakes her head. "You read my diary. You

know my old life is not something to be missed."

I scratch, "People."

"Yes, I miss people. But not all people. It's Papa I love."

I reach out to scratch the dirt again, but she catches my paw.

"I'll come back."

I shake her hand off and scratch out, "3 weeks." That's how long I gave her father. He did it; she can do it.

Belle nods.

We spend the rest of the day separate. I wonder how she will travel. I wonder what she will tell her father, her brothers, her sisters. I can't stand my worries. They don't suit my lion nature.

So I hunt.

I catch a beaver, of all things, a foolish youngster who somehow wandered too far from the pond. His top teeth cut bone-deep into my foreleg. I would eat him whole, but then I remember the hearth Belle built. I carry him home.

Chou Chou and Belle attend to me in their own ways, Belle swabbing the wound and pouring wine on it with an ironic little smile, happy to have found a use for the spirits, Chou Chou licking my face a thousand times. That night we eat beaver outside by the hearth. But Belle and I are not really together for the meal—for we are both lost inside our heads. We don't read after dinner. We pray, then sleep.

I dream of hunting in the desert of my childhood, with so many *taziyan*—greyhounds. It is a strange dream, and I'm aware of its strangeness even as I dream it, for I never hunted in my youth. The thrill of this dream hunt makes me ache. The *taziyan* bark. I'm so excited, I could bark myself. But now the dogs are barking at me, they're running at me, teeth bared, eyes hot.

I wake, shaking, and wait for dawn.

In the morning Belle comes down with the cloth sack full. "I'd like to bring presents to my family."

Her family. People. Chou Chou and I, we are not family, despite the hearth she built.

She mounts my back, but I don't know where to go. When she doesn't speak, I head for town.

At the usual spot, she dismounts. She bends to my ear and says, *"Je suis désolée"*—I'm sorry. She leaves without a backward glance.

I watch her go. Then I settle low to the ground to wait.

Within an hour, Belle appears on horseback, riding with the authority of someone who has ridden for years. She glances up toward the woods, toward where I lie hidden, but she doesn't wave. She gallops off.

CHAPTER TWENTY-TWO

At Last

Twenty-one days are a long time. I knew that, from the last time I waited. But this time twenty-one has grown.

I pass the days in projects. I kill twenty-one ducks and set about plucking them with my teeth. Chou Chou thinks this is a strange and wonderful new game. I keep moving my body between him and the pile of ducks, to keep him from ruining my plans, but though his lame leg slows him down, his persistence is remarkably effective. Finally, in defeat, I give him a duck for himself. He runs around the castle, battering the thing against the legs of chairs and tables, shaking his head and sneezing as the fluff flies. He growls and drops the duck and runs away and then comes racing back to pounce on it fiercely. I imagine Belle's laughter if she could see him.

The feathers and down from the other twenty ducks sit in a corner of Belle's room, waiting for her to make a fine new quilt so she'll be warm in the coming damp of winter. The duck bodies hang in the smokehouse, gradually turning dark. I feed the fire with green wood several times a day. The smoke stings my eyes and makes me cough. But Belle and I will be able to enjoy these together in the winter, when it's too cold to eat by the outside hearth.

I gather wood, dragging fallen trees from the forest up to the castle into a ramshackle pile. Chou Chou naturally decides this is his mountain, and he climbs to the top and yaps. Every time I toss another branch on the pile, he jumps off and runs for cover. But within moments he returns and resumes his spot of royalty.

Some branches crack easily in my jaws, so I can make their length match the fireplace. The larger ones have to lie in wait for Belle to use the ax on them. I don't know if she can swing an ax, though the way she rode that horse makes me think she can do many things I haven't guessed. But just in case, I gather a huge amount of smaller branches.

The best thing I do, though, is prepare the garden. Belle loves fresh fruits; I watched her eat cherries and raspberries with closed eyes. For some odd reason, with the exception of figs, the castle lacks fruit trees. So I'm making a mixed orchard by taking young trees from orchards nearby. Morello cherries and medlars, sour apples, pears, peaches, apricots. I even plant lemons and oranges from farms along the east coast. I don't know if they can all grow side by side, but I place the lemons and oranges on the southeast corner of the orchard, to give them the best chance. I long for banana trees and date palms, like at home, in Persia. But I haven't found any here.

Laying out the orchard is a welcome diversion. The garden is symmetrical around a central area. In the spring I will dig a small pool there and line it with stones. But, for now, Belle will have to imagine the water.

The orchard takes over much of the land nearest the castle, so I have to replant the flower gardens. But that's a joy in itself, for I remember colors vividly. I plant anemone around the bases of apricots; marigolds around the bases of pears; larkspur around the bases of sour apples. I scatter bluebells everywhere. And I make paths going out in spokes from the central area, paths lined with rosebushes.

It is not a grand garden. It is nothing compared to the scale of the gardens at my palaces in Persia. But it has charm. The colors will blend. The aromas will blend. And the fruit will satisfy. Belle will be happy here.

I work feverishly for these three weeks, proud to

have so much in place by the day of her return.

That night I open all the windows and let the smell of jasmine wet the air. I sit on my haunches on the front step and wait.

Night grows deep fast. There's a slight chill. Belle shouldn't travel alone in such darkness.

She doesn't come.

Hours pass, and she doesn't come.

That's good. She's spending the night somewhere safe.

It's morning, and she'll come now. Just one day late.

But she doesn't.

She doesn't come all day. All night.

Now she's two days late.

I'm thirsty. I haven't moved since the night Belle was due back. I go to the moat and drink. I perform the *wudhu* and pray. Then I return to the step and wait, sitting on my haunches, ready.

Days pass. Nights pass.

It rains on and off.

I don't eat, I don't drink. I drift in and out of sleep, always on my haunches. Thought is often absent, and, when it comes, it yields easily to delirium.

Chou Chou jumps at me and tries to get me to play. He whines. I know he's not suffering—for he eats his share of moles and mice. But he won't stop pestering me.

I snarl.

Chou Chou screams and runs behind a bush. After a long while, he peeks out.

And now I realize: Chou Chou does know that I attacked him that time. He knows. And he forgave me.

The knowledge makes me sadder than I have ever been before. I sink to a lying position and let my head fall on the stone step.

Chou Chou comes over and licks my ears. Inside and out. Then he falls asleep, curled against my belly.

Daylight comes. Darkness comes.

I'm not even thirsty anymore.

Once upon a time, what seems like another lifetime ago, I planned to lure a woman here so that she could love me and break the *pari*'s spell. Now that plan doesn't matter at all. I would gladly remain lion forever, if only Belle would return.

Belle is gone.

I feel myself contract, wither. Life ebbs.

I felt this way once before—on the mountain in India, when I thought of giving up. That time I got close to euphoria. This time I should make it all the way there. For if the poets of *tasawwuf*—Islamic mysticism—are right, all is happening as it should: The lover is annihilated by the beloved.

From somewhere comes the energy to walk. I go to the new orchard, to the center. Chou Chou runs ahead of me. He disappears down a hole. He's made a tunnel right here, right in the middle of my gift to Belle.

I dig at the tunnel opening. It leads to a shallow den. I dig it big enough for me, and let myself drop into it.

My thoughts are sharper now than they have been for days. I remember the old lion I met in India. The one whose ribs showed. The one I knew the jackals would chase away if I tried to leave him the meat. I see the weariness in his eyes. It is my weariness.

And now I realize I made a mistake. I should have broken off branches of roses to throw down into Chou Chou's den. Then I could have rested on a bed of thorns with rose perfume filling my head as I died.

But I haven't the strength to get up again.

I close my eyes.

"Where are you?" The voice comes from far away, high and sweet. "Oh, Mon Ami, where are you?"

A phantasm of a voice. This must be what the poets call ecstasy. I wait for my mind to explode.

Chou Chou goes running.

And the voice realizes itself into the vision of the woman. But Chou Chou jumps on her insistently. He knows this is no vision.

Belle is here, really here. She rushes along a rose path, following the fox. She kneels before me, bringing all the sweetness of a perfect rose. "What's this?

You're sick." Her face crumples with grief. "You're dying."

I stretch my paw and scratch in the dirt, "Dead long ago."

"What do you mean?"

I have no energy to explain.

Belle waves her arms around at the trees and flowers. "I have seen all that you did while I was gone — the ducks, the feathers, the firewood. I'm astonished at this garden. You make beauty." She puts both hands on my head and circles them around the backs of my ears.

"You pet me like animal."

Belle shakes her head in confusion at the words in the dirt. "But you are an animal."

A cry comes from deep in my throat. My heart breaks. I scratch out, "Not animal — monster."

Belle's eyes fill with tears. "You have a good heart, Mon Ami. You aren't a monster." She puts her hands under my chin and brings her face close to mine. "Oh, Mon Ami. I'm the one who's a monster." Her tears fall on my nose. "Forgive me for having come back late. It was hard to leave Papa, he ails so. But I had to come back."

"Why?"

"I missed everything about this new life," she says softly. "The gardens and castle. Chou Chou. Reading and praying together." She rests her chin on the top of my muzzle. "I missed you, Cher Ami. You are gentle and passionate at once. You make me happy." Her hands press. "And, most of all, you need me like no one ever has before."

All pride flames and turns to ash. The world comes alive in colors that never before existed. I need you, Belle. Oh, how I need you.

"You let me help you; you let me know you." Belle whispers now. "You let me love you."

The words seep into my head, they grow hot and loud, louder and louder, they deafen me, and I'm screaming screaming.

But it's Belle who's screaming, not me. Her hands grasp at the air.

And I catch them in mine—in my own hands. Human hands. Me, I am me. I pull Belle close and hold her fast against the impossible knowledge.

And we weep, together. Shaking.

Belle and I. Human tears for human love.

And we bow to the Merciful One and make a pool of our tears in the middle of this garden.

A pool in His honor.

The story of Beauty and the Beast recurs in fairy tales around the world. The one Americans are perhaps most familiar with has its roots in France in the 1700s, with a romance for adults written in 1740 by Gabrielle Susanne Barbot de Gallon de Villeneuve called *La jeune amériquaine, et les contes marins*, the first-known literary version of the tale. Madame Le Prince de Beaumont offered the first version for children in 1756, and it became the classic model for the tale as we know it. Indeed, popular versions of the tale, with varying styles, proliferated. Charles Lamb's poetry version in 1811 is told with propriety and civility, and it reveals that the beast had been transformed by a wicked fairy. While earlier versions also attributed the transformation to a fairy, Lamb's version named the beast-man Prince Orasmyn, and said that he was from Persia.

Given the importance of gardens in Persian history and culture—especially the importance of roses—mixed with the place the lion holds in Persian folklore, the choice of which version of the story to use as a springboard was obvious.

Thank you, Charles Lamb.

Many non-English words are used in this story, usually to give a sense of time and place. When the meanings of these words are necessary to understanding the plot, these meanings are given in the text.

However, some readers might enjoy a glossary of the words that are dearest to Orasmyn's heart.

abghosht: mutton, white beans, and spinach stew

adhan: call to prayer

anar: pomegranate

aqrab: scorpion

bade gule sourkh: the wind of roses (a particular wind that blows at the end of winter and signals the coming of spring)

bagh: garden

baghbanha: gardeners

beh daneh: quince seed

belaq: sacred garden (ancient term, lost today)

bholsari: a plant which blooms off-white in the rains

chador: veil

chambeli: a plant which blooms white, yellow, and blue in the rains and sometimes in winter

derakhte badam: almond tree

djinn: fairy

esfenaj surkh kardeh: spinach with onions and turmeric

fessenjan ba morgh ya goosht: chicken with walnut, onion, and pomegranate

ghorme sabzi: meat stew

gul: flower, rose

gule sourkh: rose (a particular kind of rose—the generic term for rose is "gule rose")

gulistan: rose garden

hajji: pilgrim

halal: prepared according to sacred custom (said of meat, similar to "Kosher" for the Jewish religion)

halim bademjan: lamb with eggplant and onions

imam: prayer leader

iwan: vaulted portal to a mosque

jannat: garden of paradise

kerna: trumpet

kuzah: a plant that blooms white in the hot season

maddi: water channel

mar: snake

mihrab: niche in a mosque wall that faces Mecca

mongra: a plant with yellow flowers in summer

muraquibah: a state of guarding, to keep away evil thoughts

naishakar: sugarcane

pari: fairy

qadi: an Islamic judge

rakat: prayer bow

riabel: a flowering plant

sabzi: spices

saz: oboe

sendjed: bohemian olive

sewti: a plant with white flowers that blooms all year, especially toward the end of the rains

sheikh: a venerable patriarch, learnéd in religion

sib: apple

sir: garlic

sophreh: cloth to eat on

souk: market

syah-dane: fennel

talar: platform

taj: crown

tanour: a flat bread

tasawwuf: Islamic mysticism (Sufism)

tawhid: the unity that bridges the distance between humans and God

taziyan: greyhounds

wudhu: cleansing ritual before prayer

zakat: charitable giving (one of the Five Pillars of Islam)

zarehun: farmers

ziyada: the outer court of a mosque

AUTHOR'S NOTE ON LANGUAGE

∾

The words in this glossary are a mix of Farsi (the language native to Persia) and Arabic (the language of Islam, which came to Persia a few hundred years before Orasmyn lived). Some of the words borrowed from the Arabic into Farsi are unaltered, whereas others have been changed as they were borrowed. In the story, many of these words appear in the plural, in which case the Farsi plural rather than the Arabic plural appears, even in Arabic words, such as *hajji*, "pilgrim," since this is the plural Orasmyn most probably would have used. So, for example, I use the Farsi plural *hajjiha* rather than the Arabic plural *hujjaj*.

A word of caution about the spelling of the words is in order. Orasmyn would have written all of these words in the Farsi alphabet or the Arabic alphabet. In the story, however, they are written in our Roman alphabet. Transliterating from other writing systems invariably results in multiple ways to spell words (that's why you've undoubtedly seen several ways to spell Hannukah, which is transliterated from the Hebrew alphabet). Whenever I dealt with Persian words in this work, I opted for a transliteration considered "ordinary" for the Iranians I have asked, even if that is not the most frequently used transliteration in the literature about Islam that I have consulted. That's because the point of view is consistently that of Orasmyn, raised with Persian traditions within a Muslim world.

Finally, a note to the budding linguists out there, who might wish there was a glossary of every non-English word in this story: Your public libraries probably have Latin and French dictionaries. I encourage you to study both a modern and an ancient language in high school if your school offers them. Language is the fabric of culture. I urge you to revel in it, as Orasmyn most assuredly did.